SOUL SONG

SOUL SONG

A STORY OF FAMILY, FAITH, AND LOVE IN THE MIDST OF ALZHEIMER'S

CONSTANCE MORRIS

WESTBOW
PRESS
A DIVISION OF THOMAS NELSON

WestBow Press books may be ordered through booksellers or by contacting:

WestBow Press
A Division of Thomas Nelson
1663 Liberty Drive
Bloomington, IN 47403
www.westbowpress.com
1-(866) 928-1240

ISBN: 978-1-4497-8857-5 (sc)
ISBN: 978-1-4497-8858-2 (hc)
ISBN: 978-1-4497-8856-8 (e)

Library of Congress Control Number: 2013904724

Printed in the United States of America

WestBow Press rev. date: 04/04/2013

Thank you to my family for all of your love and support. I am so blessed to have you in my life.

To my friends who have walked with me on this journey, I am so grateful.

To God Be All Glory

TABLE OF CONTENTS

PREFACE

There is a center in each of us, a place where we find comfort, and uniquely feel peace. For many, this place of soul is spiritual and can be triggered through prayer or meditation. A favorite song, the cadence of waves rolling or the song of a bird can initiate a journey toward this center of calmness.

I am normally not so philosophical, but life experience has brought me to this place of introspection. Those of you who have cared for someone with a long term illness can most likely relate. When those who are ill are distressed, finding their calm center can comfort them and strangely enough, those of us who care for them as well.

My mother developed Alzheimer's at a young age. She, and we, struggled with this disease for twenty-two years. Our family learned over the years how to love her through each stage of the disease. In her final years, as she became mostly non-responsive, her center of calm was sometimes the only place we could penetrate.

Soul Song is a book about a daughter's soulful journey through her mother's last days of Alzheimer's. This book is filled with struggle, diligence, commitment, compassion, faith, love and family. Although this book is fiction, and any likeness to real characters unintended, the journey portrayed is real.

My hope and prayer is that each of you who read this book will be touched. Not by the pain of this dreadful disease, although that is mostly inevitable, but by the level of richness that can be ours when we commit to faith, family and unconditional love for each other.

PART 1

ETERNITY AWAITS

1 Corinthians 2:9-10

⁹However, as it is written: "No eye has seen, no ear has heard, no mind has conceived, what God has prepared for those who love him" ¹⁰but God has revealed it to us by his Spirit.

THE WEDNESDAY
BEFORE EASTER

CHAPTER 1

I jolt back to the here and now and look in to my mother's eyes, only to see a vacant gaze. For the thousandth time, I wonder what my mother sees, what penetrates the fog that has become her existence?

Once again Becky Kennedy had been remembering another time, a time when her mother, Gloria Bridges, was a vibrant, beautiful woman. Loved and admired by everyone for her grace, her love and her God given talent. With a smile as big as Texas she could warm the inside of an ice house.

But today, she is frail and absorbed in the fog of Alzheimer's. Robbed of all but the here and now, she is a shell of her former self. She lies on her bed quietly, fidgeting with the hem of the blanket between her thumb and forefinger; back and forth, back and forth. If she knows that I am in the room, it is her own secret.

I reach over and hold her hand. Her paper-thin skin is a soft shell for the blue-veined fingers that still have a grip on her blanket. Mom manages to put a slight pressure on my thumb, diverting her blanket rub for the moment.

"I love you Mom," I say. "I love you very much." I don't know whether she understands me or not but if there is an awareness of comfort for her lonely place, I want to give her that.

"Would you like for me to sing some hymns?"

My mother was the church pianist and organist, along with the work-week role of church secretary. She loved all kinds of music, but hymns were her favorite. "Which hymn would you like to hear Mom?" I know there will be no verbal response. I haven't heard my mother say my name in over seven years or speak at all in probably five. You see, this is our twenty-second year of this dreadful disease.

"Let's sing Dad's favorite, "How Great Thou Art."" As I begin this old favorite hymn, I feel my mother grip just a little harder on my thumb. I know she hears me and I know that this is a place of comfort for her, a place where hopefully the melody penetrates the fog and comfort settles if only for the present moment.

"...Then sings my soul, my savior God to thee..."

As I sing the chorus, a single tear threatens to roll down my cheek and I rub my eye quickly. I never want her to see me cry, but the Lord knows that I have shed buckets on many days when I have left this place.

My cell phone penetrates the calm. I glance over and see that my father is calling. I pick up the phone and attempt a cheerful greeting. "Hi, Dad. How are you?"

"I am sensational today sweetheart. How is your Mom?"

"She is doing well today. We were singing a tune when you called."

Our entire family knows that "doing well" is relative and means that Mom hasn't developed a fever, doesn't have a urinary tract infection, and has made an attempt at eating her pureed food this morning.

My father, Dan Bridges, is a remarkable man. Upbeat, devoted and caring, his purpose in life has transformed from a successful businessman to a devoted husband and caretaker. Even though Mom has been in the nursing home for the last four years following her third stroke, Dad is here every day; most days two or three times a day. His love and devotion to her is a witness to *in sickness and in health*", words that are sometimes spoken only casually in marriage vows.

"I was just getting ready to leave and head back to the office Dad," I say as I lean over to give Mom a good-bye kiss. "I have about an hour before I am supposed to meet Amelia for lunch. Would you like to join us at Captain Harry's?"

Dad replies as I knew he would, "No, I plan to come over and feed your mother lunch today, but maybe a rain check. Tell Amelia I love her and to hurry up with those wedding plans. I am getting anxious!"

I can tell by the tone of his voice that he has a big grin on his face. I can see it now. Handsome and rugged, in an executive sort of way, Dan Bridges is a man whose personality fills the room. In their day, he and Mom were like a magnet. Happy, successful, and faithful to God, family and friends, no one was ever a stranger for more than a few minutes.

As I walk out the door of Mom's room, I flip the page of the guestbook. Mom and Dad have made many friends over the years and Mom continues to be blessed by the occasional visit of a friend, church member, or clergy. I have maintained the guestbook so we know who visits and can thank them when the opportunities arise. *The sign next to the book is getting tattered*, I think to myself. *I should make a new one and bring it down.*

The inscription reads; *Thank you for visiting our Mother. If she could tell you, she would be so grateful that you took time to come and see her today. Please sign our guestbook and accept our love and appreciation for this time that you have spent with her.*

CHAPTER 2

After a quick stop at the office and a few calls to confirm appointments for the afternoon, I walk into Captain Harry's and immediately see Amelia waiting on the deck that overlooks the bay. This is one of our favorite lunch spots and this beautiful April day in southwest Florida cannot be over-stated. With a canvas of blue sky overhead and a sparkling sea, we are no doubt truly in paradise.

Amelia sees me as I approach. The oldest of my two daughters, she is a beautiful combination of her father and me. Tall, lean and blonde, her blue eyes literally dance when her dimpled smile lights up her face. She is a daughter that any mom would be so proud to have. Striking on the outside; and beautiful on the inside, she is a true joy.

"Hi Mom, you look great! I love that top." I look down and I love my new top too. A pale shade of aqua, its cotton sheen shines in the sunlight. "Your eyes are so blue when you wear that color."

Amelia looks stunning in a cobalt blue sundress. "Thank you. How are you today?"

We find a table and Amelia immediately begins running through the wedding plans. Amelia will get married on June 2, just two short months away. Organized to the hilt, she has all of her plans, appointments and budget in her tablet computer. She pulls this out of her hand bag and begins going over all of the things that need to be finalized by the end of April, just two weeks away. Her final dress fitting, confirmation on the flower selection, mailing of the invitations (the Save the Date cards went out at Christmas), and the bridesmaid gifts.

I watch her, animated as she talks through her choices and the few inevitable obstacles that pop up when you are planning one of the biggest events of your life and hosting a party for one hundred fifty people.

We decide on pearl strands for the bridesmaids and select a pale pink color. Amelia has managed to pull the choices up via wireless connection to two of the shopping channels. We look through their selections and prices, finally selecting a beautiful eighteen inch strand necklace with a diamond pave clasp. A great price and a thoughtful gift; one more thing checked off of the "to do" list.

As we eat our salads, Amelia updates me on her fiancé's progress with his "to-do" list. Craig Temple is the lucky man who will spend his life with this charming daughter of mine. Craig is a good guy, and adores Amelia. Occasionally his ego is front and center, but I try to recognize that he is my daughter's choice and move on. As I reminisce about the most recent of those occasions, I realize that Amelia has just asked me a question. I refocus on her, realizing that this is the second time today that I have lost the present while cruising down memory lane. I really have to get a grip!

Amelia is looking at me expectantly and I have to respond with, "I am sorry honey. What did you ask?"

"Mother, where is your mind? This is important!"

Once I am caught up, I realize her view of important is all about how to limit her attire for the honeymoon trip to Cancun. As she recounts her dilemma, I suggest that she reduce her shoes from nine (yes, *nine* pair of shoes for a week) down to seven, as well as limit her evening attire to six ensembles instead of the ten she has listed. She is balking at the reduction, but considering the potential for bringing home souvenirs and a boutique find or two, she finally agrees that these may be reasonable options.

As we are finishing our meal, Craig rings her cell phone. He is a pilot for Skyway Airlines, a private charter company in Florida.

He has just landed in Washington D.C. with his client of the day, a well-known congressman from Florida. As she speaks to Craig, I wonder why our congressmen are not flying discount commercial. Hopefully the ride is on his personal dollar, not our tax dollars. Oh well, no time to go down that path. I have to get back to work.

I wave Amelia up from the table with a hand gesture and we walk out of the restaurant while she continues talking to Craig. From her end of the conversation, I can tell that he was originally supposed to be home tonight but from the sound of it, he will be flying to Nashville to pick up another client and fly them to Las Vegas. Home tomorrow afternoon, unless another schedule change comes his way. Amelia takes it all in stride. After dating Craig for two years she is accustomed to the schedule changes and rolls with them. That is a good thing, since her job as a trauma nurse in the emergency room is on a variable shift with many unpredictable demands. Between the two of them, actually occupying one residence after marriage will leave many days and nights away from each other.

As we head to our separate cars, Amelia yells across the parking lot asking about her sister, Adrienne. I reply that I have not heard from Adrienne today, but will be picking her up this Friday for the Easter weekend.

Adrienne is Amelia's younger sister by almost three and a half years. Night and day, fire and ice; my two daughters could not be more different. And I celebrate both of them. I realize I am so blessed to have them and to share in their diverse lives.

As I drive back to the office, I am looking forward to this weekend. My daughters will be here with me celebrating the most blessed time of year. My cell phone rings and breaks the peace of the moment. The caller ID shows Dad's number.

"Hey Dad, what's up?"

As I listen to my father's urgent voice, I make a U-turn; away from the office and toward the nursing home; to Mom.

CHAPTER 3 ▬▬▬▬▬▬▬▬▬▬▬

D ad is standing in the covered area of the driveway at the nursing home when I arrive. He hurriedly walks over to my car and asks me to drive him to the emergency room. He explains that they have taken Mother in the ambulance to the hospital. As we drive, Dad updates me on the details.

Earlier, when he entered Mother's room to feed her lunch, there was several medical staff standing around her bed. One of the nurses explained to him that although Mother typically has high blood pressure, her blood pressure had fallen dramatically. In the fifteen minutes between the routine vital taken and the charge nurse's examination; Mother was unconscious. She was covered in red spots resembling hives and after evaluation by the charge nurse, she determined that mother most likely had sepsis, an infection usually caused by bacteria.

We arrived at the hospital and I dropped Dad off at the ER entrance and went to park. I called Amelia and got her voice mail. I left her a quick message to call me that it was important, and made my way to the ER entrance.

One of the things that unfortunately we have had to learn to deal with is the medical ups and downs. Over the last twenty years, the trips to area hospitals are too many to count. As I make my way to the hospital entrance, I ring my sister's cell phone.

Laura Cox is almost three years older than me. At 57, she is in that season of life where the children are gone and thankfully you still feel good enough to enjoy yourself. Her very successful husband has taken great care of her over the years and she has blossomed as a wife and mother. Although she graduated from college and further received her Master's degree in literature, Laura has never worked outside of the home. Except that is, for the innumerable charities and causes that she supports with her time, her enthusiasm and her wealth.

Laura answers on the first ring, sounding out of breath. "Hi, Becky, I hope this is a social call in the middle of the day and everything is okay with Mom."

Boom, not surprising she is right on target. We have done this so many times. We are anxious if the phone rings at an odd time of day for a particular caller. Sad, but unfortunately, there has been much water under the bridge that brings us to this place of slight dread that something is wrong every time the phone rings.

"Unfortunately Sis, Mom has just been taken to the hospital. I am not sure how bad it is, but I will keep you posted. Early diagnosis is possibly a bacterial infection, maybe sepsis."

"Oh no, this must be pretty bad if they took her to the hospital by ambulance. Mom has urinary tract infections often. They don't land her in the hospital."

I then decide to go ahead and tell her that Mom is unconscious, something I may have waited a bit longer to share since Laura is ten hours away by car in Atlanta. It may seem harsh to hold on to this type of information, but the reality is that medical issues during our mother's illness have been frequent and often severe. I know that it is more difficult to live far away and so I try to create fewer burdens for her when I can. Just as I am about to tell her, Amelia's number comes in on the caller ID. I promise Laura that I will give her a call back as soon as I know something.

Laura and I both know the best thing for us is to get Amelia here if possible. She is the medical expert in the family and invaluable when it comes to communicating with physicians and educating us on mother's status and care options.

"Amelia thanks for calling me back so quickly. Mom has been taken to Holy Cross Hospital and I am hoping that you can come up to the ER," I say, knowing that she does not go back to work until tomorrow morning at 7:00 am. Although Amelia does not work at Holy Cross, she does know some of the staff and will be able to help us navigate the next few hours.

"I am on my way Mom. Tell Grandma to hang on and tell Granddad that I love him."

I walk into the ER and am immediately hit with the air conditioning. It must be sixty-five degrees in this place. I see Dad ahead, hands in pockets and head down. I know he is in the midst of prayer, for my mother's well-being and for his strength as he deals with the next few hours. I love him for that devotion. I start my own conversation with God as I head down the hallway toward Dad.

A few moments later as I see Amelia coming up the hallway, Dr. Jefferson, the attending ER physician comes out to the waiting area to speak with us. He reports that Mother is conscious, but early lab results show a significant infection that has created the sepsis and he is listing her in critical condition. He is candid with us and tells us that the next few hours will be indicative of whether she is strong enough to battle this new rival amidst her frail system. He indicates that he will keep her heavily sedated and on an aggressive course of antibiotics to see if she can overcome the quick decline experienced this morning. He also states that he will place her in PCU instead of ICU so that we can sit with her. He cautions us to limit her tactile exposure to us and our exposure to her over the next few hours. Amelia inquires about any organ damage or any other adverse effects that we may expect. Dr. Jefferson responds that at this time he is hoping for survival but does caution that kidney failure or other complications can occur over the next twelve to thirty-six hours.

We are experienced at waiting. There is not a waiting room in the county where we have not spent hours and days, hoping and praying on the healing grace of our Heavenly Father. On this day however, no one wants to be in the waiting room. At the moment, we are too stressed, with too much adrenaline to sit down. While we wait for Mom to be moved to her PCU room, we pace and silently pray.

I excuse myself from the room and go outside to call Laura back. Amelia is on my heels as I make my way to the parking lot, out of the air conditioning, but still shivering. It is the shivering of nerves firing in response to this change of events. Laura's phone is ringing.

"Tell me what's going on" she says as she picks up the phone. I explain to her all of the details that have been provided by the doctor. Laura has already spoken with her husband Bob Cox, and she is packing a bag. She will be on the 6:00 pm flight out of Atlanta and will arrive at the Sarasota airport at 7:20 pm. Amelia is signing to me that she will pick her Aunt Laura up and bring her to the hospital and I relay those plans to Laura. As we finish up the last minute details Laura asks if she can pray with us before we hang up. I put my cell phone on speaker and Laura begins.

"Heavenly Father, we thank you for your presence in our lives and your healing hand. We praise you God and place our love and trust in You. Be with our Mother and Father as we face the next few hours. Be with each of us and help us Lord to be strong for each other through the love and strength that you have placed in our hearts. Amen."

Amelia and I each echoed "Amen" and hung up with Laura. She was going to call her three children, Robert, Alicia and Christopher, to let them know that she was on her way to Florida and for each of them to stand-by for news.

Another thing our family understood; "stand-by." Mother had been near death several times and at other times very ill. Our family never stopped the vigil, waiting on news.

I look at Amelia as I begin dialing Adrienne's number. She isn't scheduled to fly home from Charlotte until Friday. We will keep that plan, but she needs to know about her grandmother. She will *want* to know about her grandmother. I reach Adrienne's voice mail and leave a vague message about giving me a call on my cell phone. After ending the call, I text her requesting that she call me. Adrienne, like the rest of the country's young adults, prefers texting to voice mail and is more likely to get the message quickly.

Sure enough, five seconds after pressing 'Send' I get a text from her telling me that she will call me in about five minutes. I persuade Amelia to go sit with her Grandfather while I wait for Adrienne's call. As I lean against a divider railing in the parking lot, I think about Adrienne. She is smart, funny, and slightly shy. Unlike Amelia, Adrienne can blend in to the room and go unnoticed for long periods of time. Adrienne prefers being at home, the comfort of a few close friends, and the tranquility of quiet. Her wavy brown hair and hazel eyes are a striking contrast. She frequently turns the head of many a young man, and yet she seldom notices any of their attentions.

The cell phone chirps Adrienne's custom ring, one she set herself on a prior visit home. As soon as I answer, she begins telling me about her day. She is in the middle of a big software contract and has less than three hours to get several of the clauses worked out.

"Mom, I hope this is important because I am really under the gun here."

I smile at her intensity. Adrienne does nothing half-way. If you own a company, you want her working for you. As a matter of fact, I have already tried to lure her my way but she has no interest in real estate law. Software is the future from her perspective.

"Adrienne your Grandmother was taken to the hospital a little bit ago and she is pretty sick."

I give Adrienne enough details to convey the seriousness of the illness, but not so much as to have her jumping on the next plane. Friday will be fine.

"Oh no," Adrienne cried. "I am so sorry, how is Granddad?"

I assure her that her grandfather is handling this as he usually does; with confident authority and faithful devotion. Adrienne gets this picture totally; having experienced her Grandfather's 'take charge' personality.

We discuss plans for the next few minutes and I assure her that she does not have to come home yet. We will see her on Friday but will keep her posted whenever we have new details. I encourage her to get back on her contract and let us take care of things here.

"I love you Mom. I will say a prayer for all of you." My sweet Adrienne, I can't wait to see her.

I turn around and walk back in to the hospital. Amelia has texted me the room number, so I head to the fourth floor, room 429.

CHAPTER 4 ▨

A melia and Dad are settled in to the hospital room but Mom still hasn't been brought up from the ER yet. Dad is running through Mom's condition in his mind as he waits, reliving her status yesterday, last night, and early this morning when he came in to feed her breakfast.

"I saw no signs of these issues just hours ago," he remarked to both Amelia and I.

It is true, the decline seemed fast. One of the difficult things about the maturity of this disease is the inability to communicate. Unfortunately, Mom can't tell us when she is feeling bad. We can't see dizziness, or feel pain for her. The symptoms that we most often look for are agitation or outward signs like a fever, chills or a change in her urine or bowel routine. I had only been gone from Mother's room an hour or two before the nurse discovered the problem. Even with our experience, the rapid onset of symptoms seems odd.

"Becky, are you sure there was nothing unusual when you were with your mother earlier?"

Before I can respond, he is on to his next question. "How much did she eat at lunch time?"

I responded that her appetite seemed normal for lunch time, usually a little less than her other meals of the day.

I can tell that Dad is having a hard time coming to grips with all of it. He always feels so responsible when these things happen. I try to reassure him that it is just one of those things and intellectually he realizes that as well, but his heart is part of her and he is restless; looking for answers where none can be found.

Once again, Dad asks Amelia to go find out where Mom is and what is taking so long. Amelia heads for the hospital room door and arches one eyebrow as she goes by, while her back is to my father. I understand the meaning of her expression which implores me to help him get a handle on this before we all get crazy. As she walks out of the room, I look at my father and see his sadness as it begins to shape his features. I have seen this before. First the adrenaline rush, then action and then reality sets in. This could be it. This could be the last time we go through this with her. Just as quickly, he shakes it off, but not before I get a glimpse of the vulnerability he has at this very moment. He and Mother will celebrate sixty years of marriage this summer. If his will power could keep her alive, she would live forever.

My cell phone rings. As I remove it from my purse, I see that it is my office calling. I answer the phone and hear Mary Martin on the line. Mary is my administrative assistant and I realize that in all of the commotion I have forgotten to let her know that I am not going to be back in the office this afternoon. I quickly brief her on Mother's condition and then answer a few urgent questions that she has on one of our cases so she can get time-sensitive documents out today.

Mary has worked with me at my law firm, Kennedy Law Group, since I opened the doors here seven years ago. My husband Roger and I built this law firm together in Tampa and had worked there for about twelve years. Once Mom's illness became so significant, Roger and I decided to open a branch here in Sun Key, just outside of Sarasota. We purchased a condo on the Gulf of Mexico and he and I both worked in Tampa a few days a week and in Sun Key a day or two a week. As Mom required more care, I began spending more time here instead of our home in Tampa.

Two years ago, Roger was killed in a car accident returning to Tampa from a long weekend at the condo. His unexpected loss was devastating to me and our girls. Roger was the love of my life and my best friend. He was a true family man. When the girls were growing up his favorite place to spend his free time was at home with us. When Amelia went off to college, Roger had as much separation anxiety as I did. When Adrienne left for college, we prepared by scheduling a trip to San Juan. The Caribbean climate and the persistent waves on the shore were the distraction we needed to bridge the onset of the empty nest.

Last year I sold the Tampa law practice to two of the senior partners and moved full time to Sun Key. Mary has been with me through it all. I truly don't know what I would have done without her.

As I disconnect the call, I hear Amelia in the hallway. She walks into the room followed by the gurney carrying Mother. As the orderlies settle Mother on the hospital bed, I walk over and put my arms around Dad. He has always been the rock for us kids, but even he needs the support once in a while.

I look at the clock and realize that it is already 4:00. Laura will be here in a few hours and it will be a relief to have her here. She is a strong, sensible woman with a kind heart. Dad and I will need her common sense approach to handle things over the next few days. Laura has always been the one who can coordinate the communication, visitors, schedules and all of the other details that come along with extended family getting together and the onslaught of caring friends that make up the network of support that my parents have in this community.

Amelia moves to the doorway of the room to see if she can catch the nurse's attention. Anxious to hear if Mom's vitals have changed, Amelia is hoping for some progress before she leaves for the airport to get Laura. The nurse confirms what we suspect. There is no change and Mom should be resting comfortably over the next few hours as her body struggles to fight the infection and its toll on her system.

As Amelia is getting ready to leave for the airport, Dad encourages me to leave as well to handle a few things at home before coming back to the hospital for what I am sure will be most of the night. I have no intention of leaving Dad at the hospital and appease him by asking Amelia to run by my house and pick up a sweater and my tennis shoes. She promises that she will and offers to stop by Dad's house and freshen the guest room for Laura. Laura will want to stay with Dad at his house, and of course I will have Adrienne coming in on Friday and she will be staying at my house.

With Amelia gone, Dad and I get comfortable, each on one of the hard vinyl hospital chairs. Without much to do for now, I prop my feet up on the bed frame and begin to check my smart phone for messages. I see another text from Adrienne looking for an update on Mom's condition. I text her back and let her know that Mom's condition is stable for now and I will keep her posted. I also have an email from our pastor. Dad must have called Reverend James while I was out talking with Adrienne. I reply back to his request to keep him posted and thank him for his prayers. Reverend Russell James and his wife Collette have been at our church for the last three years. They have become family to us and we are so grateful for their leadership and support over these difficult times with Mother.

I address a few other business related messages and then open a solitaire game on the device to keep my mind active. After winning two and losing one, I put the phone away and offer to get Dad a cup of coffee. He requests a cola and something sweet, so I head down to the cafeteria.

I carry pomegranate green tea bags in my purse and right now that sounds perfect to me. In the cafeteria, I find a piece of coconut crème pie for Dad and manage to carry his pie, cola and my hot water back to the room.

When I arrive one of our close friends, Maxine Banks is in the room with Mom and Dad. Maxine has been friends with them for the last 30 years. She is the closest thing to family that we have and

I give her a hug. She offers to give up her chair but I encourage her to stay seated. Standing up and stretching feels great and Maxine has her own health issues to deal with.

As Dad and I visit with Maxine, Amelia walks back in the room with an overnight bag for me; my sweater and shoes tucked inside. She is on her way to the airport but knows that I will be cold and uncomfortable without them. Amelia reaches over and gives Maxine a hug and kiss. She and Adrienne have always called Maxine "Aunt Maxine". She loves my daughters like they were her own granddaughters and they love her back.

Amelia is off again almost as quickly as she came; wanting to be sure that she makes the forty-five minute drive to the airport in time to greet Aunt Laura's flight. It is already 5:45, so she needs to get on the road soon. On her way out she promises that she will text us as soon as she and Aunt Laura are headed back to the hospital.

It has been a long day, especially for Dad. As the room becomes quiet again, Dad doses in his chair. Maxine and I sit in peaceful silence, each lost in our own thoughts about life, sickness, family and faith.

After a half hour or so, Maxine gets up to leave and puts her forefinger over her lips to signal her intention on a quiet exit. As I quietly stand, Dad opens his eyes, on edge for any change in sound in the room. He sees Maxine out and gives her a hug. He promises to let her know if anything changes and she assures us that she will check in tomorrow.

CHAPTER 5

L aura and Amelia arrived at the hospital around 9:30. Laura's flight landed a few minutes late and the luggage carousel was delayed.

After hugs shared, Laura walks over to Mom's side and reaches for her hand. Although we have been cautioned on exposure, no one is going to stop Laura from holding Mom's hand for a few minutes. Laura has not been down to Florida since Christmas and she stares at Mom for a few minutes, tears forming in the corner of her eyes.

I reflect and realize that I can't remember whether Mom has declined in her appearance since Christmas. Since I see her almost daily, it is hard to place a timeframe on how her features change over time.

Laura tells Mom she loves her and Dad steps up to put his arm around Laura. She gives Dad another hug and he offers her his chair. Amelia steps out in the hall to see if she can find another couple of chairs for the room. Since Mom has this infection, she has been assigned a private room. Amelia comes back with two chairs and we all sit in a circle around the bed.

We fill Laura in again on all of the details of Mom's status. Amelia reviews the chart at the door to catch up on any new information and heads down the hall to speak with the nurse. When she returns, she lets us know that Mom's internal medicine physician, who has cared for her for years, is reading the chart and will be in to see Mom shortly.

Dad is encouraged by this and all of our focus is trained on the door of the room waiting for Dr. Hill to arrive. Within minutes he greets each of us and walks over to the bed to examine Mom. After a brief exam, including pupil reaction and reflexes, he confirms his support of the diagnosis given by the ER physician. He restates what we have already heard; the sepsis is most likely due to a bacterial infection from the bladder which could have been caused by many things. He notes that although they have her sedated with medication, she is conscious, just not awake. He also cautions that this is serious and the prognosis "guarded" at best.

We thank Dr. Hill and wait until he has left the room. As I knew he would, Dad turns to Amelia.

"Amelia, we all know what the doctors say. Is there anything else we should know about this before we lift up your Grandmother in prayer? I want to be specific with our requests."

"Granddad, she is a fighter. This sepsis is scary stuff, and Grandma is frail, but we have seen her come through these things before and we must have caught this early since both you and Mom were with her just hours before."

Dad looked at Amelia closely and then said, "Alright then. Let's take this to God." As Dad prepared to pray, we each held another's hand and put our other hand on Mom's legs.

"Heavenly Father, we are here again with you, the Master Healer. Gloria is very sick Lord, you know her condition better than we do and you alone know whether or not she is on the edge of your Kingdom. Lord we pray for your mercy on her comfort, and your will on her healing. We ask you to bless our family as we come together again to show her our love and to support each other in whatever we must face over the next few days. Lord you know we love her, and we know you love her too. If it is your will, show her favor in solid healing and bring her back to us. We ask this in your Holy Name, Amen."

As I listen to this passionate prayer, I cannot help the tears rolling down my face. I am always moved by my father's heartfelt prayers and candid devotion to our Lord and our Mother. It is a beautiful thing.

As I look up, I am not the only one. Amelia's blue eyes are magnified by the tears found there and Laura has lost some of her eyeliner in paths down each side of her face. We are a soppy bunch, but I am so aware of how special these times can be and grateful for the strength of this family bond.

It is just past 11:00 pm and I convince Amelia to go home so that she can get some rest before her shift tomorrow. Amelia works ten hour shifts, four days a week and her shift begins tomorrow. Fortunately she is scheduled to be off on Friday when Adrienne arrives, but unfortunately is scheduled to work on Easter. Her time with Adrienne will be limited, but we will try to get as much together time as possible over the next few days.

Shortly after Amelia leaves, I suggest to Dad that he take Laura home and get her settled. I offer to cover the first overnight shift (it has never occurred to us not to cover twenty-four hours a day with Mom in the hospital). Mom cannot call out for help, ring a nurse call bell, or signal in any way if she is in distress. Leaving her alone is not an option.

"Alright, Laura and I will go to the house if you will promise me that you will call immediately if there is any change."

"I promise Dad. You know I will call you."

As I hug Laura and Dad good-night, I am grateful to have family to lean on during times like these. Handling this without them would be so difficult.

CHAPTER 6

A s I begin to settle in for the night, I look in the overnight bag that Amelia brought to me on the off chance that she has packed a toothbrush and a pair of socks. I rely on her organization and her initiative to go beyond the request of just a sweater and shoes, and I am not disappointed. Not only do I have socks and a toothbrush, but she has also packed my Bible and my hymn book. Amelia knows that I love to sing to Mother and although I know all of the words to most verses of any hymn, she knows that I find comfort in reading the words. How thoughtful of her.

I brush my teeth, accept a blanket from the night nurse, and place two chairs facing each other so that I can prop up my feet and maybe lightly nap if I am lucky. I reach for the hymnal and look up the song that has been playing in the back of my mind all afternoon. I look over at Mother and she is sleeping, in the same position she has been all afternoon except when the nurses have moved her to reduce the pressure on her skin.

I begin to sing quietly, and move my foot from the chair to the bed so that I can place my foot next to hers. The song that has played in my mind becomes music to my lips;

"When peace like a river, Attendeth my way.
When sorrows like sea billows roll,
Whatever my lot, Thou has taught me to say,
It is well, It is well, with my soul."

I love this old hymn. Many don't know the story of the writer, Horatio Spafford. Horatio was a real estate attorney in the mid-late 1800s in Chicago. He wrote the song after several tragedies struck his family, understanding that we all will experience death and our preparation for this transition is about our soul. What an incredible insight on his part. As I sing the last verse, the potential timing of its message is not lost on me. One thing I know for sure, my Mother's soul will be in heaven and her celebration will be sweet as a result of her preparation here on earth.

> "O Lord hath the day, When my faith shall be sight,
> The clouds be rolled back as a scroll.
> The trump shall resound, and the Lord shall descend,
> Even so, it is well with my soul."

As I finish this incredible song, I am reminded of Psalm 34:19; *"A righteous man may have many troubles, but the Lord delivers him from them all."*

When my mother leaves this life, she will no longer have the suffering of this terrible disease. That is such an amazing blessing. I know if she were awake today, and could communicate, she would tell me that she cannot wait to be a part of eternity.

As I look at my mother, I think about this journey. None of us could ever have imagined the duration or the toll that this disease would take on my mother and our family. I look at the woman lying on the bed and reflect on the absence of essentially all of my mother's characteristics. My mother was vibrant, not immobile; caring, not confused; beautiful, not pale and failing. Although I love the person in this bed because she is my mother, I truly miss the woman that I remember her to be. It has been so long and so painful to watch her lose the battle with this mind-robbing disease.

I reflect back on all of the stages that we have gone through and understand that we have been living and experiencing a grief process for over twenty years. We began with denial of the problem, then anger at the circumstance, followed by sadness at the reality and finally acceptance of the condition. But with each stage of function loss comes another round of grieving.

I think about my friends and how involved their mothers have been in their lives and in their children's lives and I am so sad. Sad that Mother didn't have that opportunity, sad that I didn't have my mother in that way and sad for my daughters who really don't remember much about their grandmother before her illness. She would have been such a positive influence on them.

I look down at my watch and notice that more than an hour has passed. I stand up and stretch. Sleep, even the desire to sleep, has escaped me. I walk to the doorway and look down the hall. For a PCU unit, where everyone here is critically ill, the place is quiet. I see two nurses in the central station and head that way. I stop at the desk and ask them if they have a bottle of water for me and mouth swabs for mother. Even though Mother cannot have any liquid in her mouth that might cause her to strangle, wetting her lips with the aloe based mint flavored swabs helps to avoid the severe dryness and chapping.

I return to Mother's room with both items and set the water bottle down next to my chair. I walk over to Mom and open one of the foils that contain the swabs. It is 1:30 am. I note the time so that I can keep track of when I first wet her lips. Probably not necessary, but I have years of experience in writing everything down so that Dad can see what has been done.

I sit back in my chair and open my Bible. I have no idea where I should start. All day long I have been mentally going back to my scriptural staple, the one that sustains me. Why can't I remember where that passage is in the Bible? Psalms, Proverbs?

"Lean not on your own understanding".

For me that has been the foundation for coping. Not just with Mother's condition, but with the tragic loss of my husband, the father of my girls. I cannot count the hundreds of times I have turned to that scripture. Surely the page is tattered in my Bible.

Finally I find it. Of course, it is Proverbs 3:5-6.

"⁵Trust in the Lord with all your heart and lean not on your own understanding; ⁶in all your ways acknowledge Him, and He will make your paths straight".

I begin to read the full chapter when I notice Mother move. She has turned her head and is looking in the corner of the room. I look up to the corner to see if there is a light or something that may have attracted her attention. Nothing is there. As I look back at Mother, she smiles, not at me but at the ceiling. I push my chair closer to the bed and lean over her to say hello and touch her forehead.

"Hi Mom, are you awake? It's Becky."

She is still smiling and looking past me to the corner. I look again to see if there is anything there, but the corner of the ceiling is dark.

As I turn back, the most remarkable thing occurs. My mother, who has not had the muscle tone to sit up in bed by herself in at least three years, is in motion to sit up. She is reaching and smiling at the corner of the ceiling to the left of her bed, the side that I am sitting on. I watch, in awe of the presence of whatever she sees, understanding that it is beyond my realm of vision.

She is in a half sit-up on the bed with her arm reaching toward the ceiling and truly the most beautiful smile on her face. It is a smile of recognition, a smile of happiness and an expression without confusion or pain. I believe, sitting right in this chair, that I am seeing my Mother's last minutes on earth. I can't help but think that her family already passed is sitting at the crossroads to heaven waiting on her.

I do not move. I am not sure I am breathing. Slowly, Mother's smile begins to fade and she gradually, with control, lies back down. She is still reaching for the ceiling corner, but the smile has gone and the confusion is back. She draws her arm back in and stares straight up at the ceiling.

When I believe the moment has passed, I lean over to her and I speak gently to her.

"Mom, who did you just see? Did someone come to see you? Was it angels or did you see Grandma and Granddad waiting for you?"

Of course she does not respond, and the distance in her eyes is back. I tell her that I love her and sit back in my chair.

I reflect on what just transpired and I know that it cannot be explained in any other way. Two things have just happened and both of them were from divine origin. My Mother saw something that brought her joy and longing, that I couldn't see, and my Mother just demonstrated physical capacity that she has not had since two strokes ago. She sat up in bed, unattended, without the use of her arms, and was able to hold that position for at least a minute. Frankly, I am not sure I could do the same thing without some serious tummy crunching.

As I look over at Mother, she is fast asleep again, knocked out by the strong antibiotics. I am in awe and I bow my head in prayer. This prayer is coming from a place that I have never experienced before. I know, beyond a shadow of doubt, I have just witnessed her touched by the life beyond. Her unbridled joy and her clear longing to reach out to whatever she saw, reinforced what I already knew. Heaven is going to be a great place. For some reason, this moment, was just not her time to go.

I reach for my Bible again, but this time I have a quest. I want to read about angels.

THE THURSDAY
BEFORE EASTER

CHAPTER 7

As I am looking up scripture and reading verses on the roles of angels, Laura walks in the room. I glance at the clock which reads 4:30 am and then back at Laura. "Couldn't sleep?" I asked.

Laura said that she was able to sleep for a little while but decided to go ahead and come down and give me a chance to go home and get some sleep.

"I figured that you would be exhausted and could use a little sleep before the decisions of the day would need to be made, whatever those might be. I took Dad's truck and left a note on the counter for him to call me whenever he wants to be picked up."

Laura probably didn't realize how out of sorts Dad would be without transportation. Not to mention that he wouldn't be happy about neither of us being here while she went back to pick him up, especially first thing in the morning when the doctors are most likely to do their rounds.

I offer to go back to Dad's and get him in a little while, knowing that he will be up early and wanting to spend the time with Mom. But first, I have to fill Laura in on the most amazing experience of my life.

Laura listened with intensity and began shaking her head as the story ended. I demonstrated for her how Mom sat up on the bed and she couldn't believe it either. We both sat next to Mom's bed and wondered if she would in fact make it through this infection. Was the vision that she had a preamble of what is to come?

I really cannot bear to leave Mother, but I know that Dad will be breathing fire if he is ready to come to the hospital and there is no ride. Fortunately, he only lives about five miles from the hospital, so I gather my things and put them back in the overnight bag and place it in the corner. I give Laura a hug and tell her that I will be back as soon as Dad is ready.

As I walk down the hall heading out of the hospital, I feel drained, but joyful. I reflect on how reassured I am that our Mother is in God's hands and I prepare myself, certain that her time on this earth is limited. Her pain and suffering have been almost too much to watch over the years and although we will be sad, there will also be relief in her final peace and comfort.

As I let myself in Dad's front door, I suddenly realize how exhausted I am. I don't smell coffee and actually wonder if he is awake. I move through the foyer and to the hall on the left toward his room. As I get near the end of the hall, I can hear his shower running in the master bath. Wow, I got here in the nick of time!

I head back to the kitchen and begin to brew coffee. Funny thing about Dad, he gets up, puts his feet on the floor and hits the shower. I would trip and fall in the shower without my very large cup of brew in the morning. Caffeine kicks start my system and even though I have now been up for 24 hours, I will pour myself a cup of that delightful bean brew.

I hear Dad coming down the hall and I call out to him to make sure he is dressed. "Dad, don't come out in your skivvies, I came home to give you a ride, not get the surprise of my life." Dad rounds the corner, shaved, showered and dressed for the day. He gives me a huge hug and a kiss on the cheek.

"How was Mom's night? Any news?"

I reply that she slept most of the night, intentionally avoiding the spiritual realm for now. I am not sure how Dad will take it. Mostly I think he will be sorry that he was not there to share it with her. That is how he is, wanting to share it all with her. It makes me cry, and I swallow the emotion that is building.

"Laura is there with her. She awoke early and decided to come down to the hospital. Of course, her only transportation was your truck." Dad looks out the kitchen door that leads to the garage and says, "I cannot believe I didn't hear her leave. You think she would tell me that she is leaving with my truck."

"Dad, she didn't want to wake you. She knew the day you had ahead and wanted you to get as much sleep as possible."

"Speaking of which, you my dear have had no sleep. Why don't you go lie down in the guest room and take a nap. I will come get you when you call me and tell me you are awake and rested."

I assure Dad that I am okay, and I really want to be at the hospital when the doctor comes for his rounds. I look at the clock and see it is just after 6:00 am. We better go if we are going to make sure we have a chance to see the doctor.

"Dad, grab your cup and let's go. You know these doctors. They visit the patients before the family comes so they don't have to answer as many questions. We are not going to let them get away with that today are we?"

"Not today. We will get a biscuit or bagel, something to eat when we get to the hospital."

As Dad gets in the driver's seat, I take a good long look at him. He will be 83 years old in July. He is a striking man, confident, proud and independent. He is in amazingly good shape and honestly never complains about what surely must be some significant aches and pains.

"How are you feeling Dad?" I am wondering how much this situation with Mom is weighing on him. "Did you get any sleep last night?"

"That is two questions. I can't even answer one before you ask another one. I am fine. I have your Mother on my mind and that is exactly how it should be. I wouldn't change a thing."

What a man . . . I see him day after day doting on Mom and I just am amazed by this gift of love that they have shared in the past and he keeps alive today. *"Thank you God for such amazing parents,"* I pray quietly.

We arrived at the hospital by 6:20 and Laura assured us when I called her cell phone to tell her that we were on our way that the doctor had not been in yet. That is a relief to Dad and he quickens his step as we enter the hospital lobby. We know from experience that missing the doctor's morning rounds can mean a day of waiting around trying to find out status, treatment plan and prognosis.

Just as we get in the elevator my cell rings. I see that it is Amelia calling and I tell Dad to go ahead without me, I will be there in a minute. Amelia is on her way to work and wants an update on Mom. I tell her that there is no change and we are at the hospital hoping to catch the doctor on his rounds.

"Amelia, if we need your input when the doctor comes in I will text your cell with MOM." That is our code word for 'call as soon as you can'. Both of our girls know that drill after so many years of Mom's illness.

Amelia promises that she will keep her cell with her and call if she can while the doctor is in the room, or at least hopefully while he is still on the floor. We say goodbye and I head up to room 429. This all-nighter that I have pulled is starting to take its toll. I remember this feeling. My brain starts to feel a little numb, my eyes are scratchy from all of the hospital dry air, and even though I brushed my teeth last night, the film on my teeth is borderline gross.

Laura and Dad are in the room when I get there, as is the charge nurse and the aid. Shift change is taking place and the next hour will be a hub-bub of activity as the watch baton is transferred from one shift to another.

Laura and I go to one side of the room so that she can update me. Mother's blood pressure is back to normal/high, and they see this as a good sign. The results of the blood work taken around 6:00

am should be available soon and we will have an idea on the levels of infection and other key issues. Of real concern is the kidney function, so those labs will be important. Mother really hasn't moved all night, other than my experience with her sitting up. Although Mom cannot sit up or roll from side to side, she does move her arms and her head under normal conditions. The concern here is the risk of pressure sores if she is not rotated. The staff seems to be pretty slack about this and I step over to the bed where the charge nurse is still recording vitals on the file.

"Roberta, we want to make sure that Mom is turned at least every two hours while she is here. If you could put that instruction on the chart we would appreciate it," I say to the charge nurse. Roberta assures me that turning non-mobile patients every two hours is a standard of care that the nurses follow.

"Well I appreciate that there are standards of care, but I can assure you our mother has not been turned every two hours. With the exception of the last hour, I have been at this hospital since Mother was admitted and I am only aware of three turns plus the one that you just did. That is only a turn every 3-4 hours. Given the number of years our mother has been bedridden, we will have bed sores in a very short period of time." I know I am stern, but patient advocacy is a serious business and family care-givers have to step up to the plate.

In the most courteous tone I am sure Roberta can muster, she assures us that these instructions will be clear to the day shift. To soften the moment, I thank Roberta and ask her to realize that we have spent many years taking care of our mother; through many hospitalizations, years of nursing home and years before that in our home. She nods her understanding and addresses my father saying, "I will let the day shift know that you want to speak to the doctor."

After Roberta and the nurse aide left the room, Laura looked at me and said, "I am glad that is you giving that speech. I don't have the velvet hammer approach that you have."

In truth, although Laura is an amazing woman, she is non-confrontive. Sometimes you just have to be assertive. Our Mother could go either way at this point, and I don't want it to be from negligence. If it is God's chosen time for her to leave, I will celebrate her life and her entrance to heaven, but not at the hand of bad care.

One would think that with a daughter as a nurse I would be easier on them, but Amelia would be the first to tell them if there is an issue and frankly would expect the same from her patient families. She has told me many times, she would rather contend with an assertive family than no family, and unfortunately many patients do not have the family support.

I excuse myself for a minute and go call the office. Mary is usually there by 7:30 and I am hoping to catch her early. Clearly, I need my appointments for the day rescheduled.

Last year, I reduced my hours at my law firm to part time as a billing attorney in order to spend more time with Mom and Dad. That has made things much easier, and frankly the only way I could have logistically rescheduled yesterday afternoon's appointments and all day today. Tomorrow, Good Friday, is a holiday for the office so Monday will be the earliest opportunity to make up for this time. I settle my thoughts now, knowing that I can spend this time with my family and then focus on my client needs next week, unless of course things don't go well for Mom.

Mary is in the office, just getting organized for the day. We go over a few details and spend several minutes on one particular urgent case. After a few more discussion items, she wishes us well today and will stay in touch if anything should come up. My practice is small, but I have three other attorneys in the office, all of whom can cover for me.

As I head back to the room, I see Laura motioning for me at Mom's door. The doctor is in the room and Mom has had some type of seizure or convulsion. Laura and Dad were in the room when it started, but the nurses quickly moved in because her blood pressure elevated significantly and the notice alarms sounded the distress at the nurse's station.

The PCU staff doctor, Dr. Waring, is in the room and has begun to review Mom's latest lab work. The infection is still very significant and there are some early signs of kidney impact, although Dr. Waring indicates that this is not at a level to be too concerned with yet. He will continue her on her medicine course and increase the IV fluids to avoid dehydration.

I step out of the room and text Amelia. Within a minute or two she rings my cell phone. I update her on Mother's condition and the physician's comments on her present status. Amelia actually knows Dr. Waring and indicates she thinks he is very competent. She is concerned by the update but confirmed his direction which is the next twenty-four to forty-eight hours will be critical.

Laura comes out of the room. She wants to call her family and give them an update. She is emotional and I give her a big hug. We will do this many times over the next few days. The strong one for the moment will rotate and I feel so blessed to have her. I know that she will feel better if her husband Bob is here and I expect that she will call him and ask him to come. Her son Robert lives in Charlotte and is married with two elementary age children. Alicia, her middle child is also married and has two toddlers. She lives in Denver and is the longest distance from the family. Chris, her youngest child, is single and lives in Atlanta.

Laura heads down the hall and I go back in to the room. Dad is clearly stressed, but talking to mother in his 'happy' tone. He believes to his core, and I agree with him, that Mom knows whether she is in a happy place or a stressed place. He feels that creating that happy atmosphere is where he can have a positive impact and show his love at the same time.

I collapse in one of the chairs and text Adrienne. I let her know that her Grandmother is still in critical condition but that we are hanging in there. She will be flying in tomorrow. Whatever the situation here, that is soon enough. Adrienne texts me back and thanks me for the update. She asks me to tell her grandfather that she loves him and she is praying for her grandmother. I read the text to Dad, and he promptly starts talking to Mom, reminding her who Adrienne is and telling her that Adrienne is praying for all of us.

"Isn't that great Gloria? We have the most special grandchildren."

My exhaustion is catching up with me and I know the emotions will follow. It is already 8:30 am. I tell Dad that I am going to go home for a few hours. He promises me that he will call me if there is any change. I give him a kiss and gather my handbag, leaving the overnight bag here. I will need it again later.

As I walk out of the room, looking for Laura to let her know that I am going home, all I can think about is a shower and a nap. I need this if I am going to be able to handle whatever comes later. My condo is about a half hour from the hospital, but since I don't have any clothes at Dad's, I have to make the trip. I will pack a few things and put them in the car so that I can freshen up at Dad's rather than drive all the way home again later.

I find Laura in the gift shop buying a diet soda. She has never been the coffee drinker that runs in the rest of the family. I give her a hug and a kiss and head out the door. I make a mental note that I want to be back here by early afternoon so that Laura can get a break. It may be our family dynamics, but we would never leave Dad alone with Mother in this condition. As strong as he is, losing our Mom will be devastating for him.

CHAPTER 8

As I get in my car to go home, I feel like I have been at the hospital for days. I maneuver the car out of the Emergency parking lot and head toward home.

I live on Sun Key, the north end of the island. Dad is on the mainland, on the south end of Sun Key. Although it is only about ten miles from Dad's house to my condo, it takes almost a half hour since the speed limit ranges from 35-45 mile per hour for that distance. In addition, the beach scene and sightseers slow Gulf Drive to a crawl, especially during Spring Break.

As I cross over the bridge to the Key, I begin to anticipate the day's events. Most likely it will be a long day of waiting. As tired as I am, it bothers me to be going home. It is hard to explain sometimes, even to myself, but I want to be there. I have a need to be there for my family. Rationally I realize that a tired Becky is of no use to anyone, but it is difficult anyway.

It is times like these that I miss Roger more than words can express. He was the calming wind beneath my wings. I wish desperately that he was home right now. That he could greet me and hold me in his arms and let me cry. I loved that about him. He wasn't one of those men that had to 'fix' everything. He could just let my emotions be expressed. He was my soft place to fall.

"Lord, I miss him. I hope you have him doing great work up in heaven because I sure miss him here."

As I navigated my way among the beach-goers, strolling shoppers, and gleeful children looking forward to the waves, I began to sing to myself.

"I surrender all. I surrender all. All to Thee my blessed Savior, I surrender all."

As I make my way through the melody, I remember that I am supposed to sing a solo this Sunday for the Easter service.

And then it dawns on me. I will never, ever sing this song the same way again after being with mother last night. My solo for Sunday is the contemporary Christian song, "*I Can Only Imagine*", by MercyMe.

As I transition to the words of that song, the Spirit of Jesus' resurrection and the life hereafter overwhelm me, but instead of being emotional like I usually am, I am joyous—almost giddy.

As I pull in to my condo development, I am ready to rest. I feel peaceful and once again, very tired. A shower, a nap and pack a bag.

It is 1:00 in the afternoon when I awake. I cannot believe that I have slept this long. Although four hours of sleep is not a lot, it is surprising that I was able to manage for that length of time. I begin to dress and pack my bag, noticing that I left my phone in my purse. I hurry to the kitchen, chiding myself the entire way. *What if something had happened? What if someone was trying to reach me?*

I retrieve my phone from the purse. Two missed calls and three texts. I hit the texts first—faster if there is new information. The first is from Bob, Laura's husband with well wishes for us. The second is from Adrienne looking for an update. The third is from Amelia letting me know that she will be coming by the hospital when she gets off at 6:00; providing she isn't held up by an emergency. I breathe a sigh of relief. If something significant had happened with Mom, Laura would have called my cell and texted me.

I check the voice mails. One is from Mary at the office with a notification of a counter-suit. Doug Andrews, one of my law associates will handle the immediate details. The second voice mail is from Doug Andrews, letting me know that he has filed the appropriate documents. He expresses his concern about Mother and tells me not to worry about anything at the office. Once again—thank goodness for great family, great business associates and great friends.

I zip my small bag and grab some clothes on hangers to take to Dad's. Although I will be bringing Adrienne back here tomorrow night, this will definitely save me some time in the next day or so. On my way out the door of the condo, I ring Dad.

"Dad—hey it is me. How is Mom?" Dad replies that they have had another seizure episode but it was not as bad as the first one. She has stabilized again and is resting. "I am on my way there. Do you need anything?"

"No honey, we are good. Laura went downstairs and got sandwiches earlier from the cafeteria. Just come on to the hospital and be with us," Dad replied. Translation after many years of co-caring for Mother with Dad; he needs me.

As I drive to the hospital, my cell phone rings. One glance at the caller ID indicates it is Pastor James. "Hello Russell."

"Hi Becky, how are you holding up?"

"I am doing well. I am headed back to the hospital after a shower and a nap."

Pastor Russell James responded, "I just left the hospital. I am glad that you have had a rest and am also happy that you are headed back that way. Your Dad is hanging in there but I think he is getting a little weary."

"Why, has anything happened that they are not telling me before I get there?"

"No, I was there when you called. I just think that your Dad realizes that the longer she fails to improve, the larger the odds are that she may not make it this time," Russell responded.

"I will be there soon. I appreciate your checking in with him this morning and as usual, yours and Collette's love and support."

"Speaking of Collette," Russell began, "she wants me to let you know that she plans to come and spend some time with you and Laura at the hospital whenever it is convenient for you. She doesn't want to intrude, but would love to be there to support you, Amelia, Laura and of course your Dad."

Collette, she is like a sister to me. I have loved getting to know she and Russell since their ministry brought them to Sun Key.

"Russell, Collette can come any time, she knows that. Both of you are like family to us."

"I will tell her Becky. You know she thinks Daniel is her second Dad and you as the sister she never had. My guess is that you can expect to see her up there later today."

"Russell, before you go, I am supposed to have the solo at church Sunday. I am still planning on it, but we need a Plan B in the event that something changes on this end." I knew that I could pull this together without much practice, but realistically, I would need some time with Grace Mitchell the organist to practice and I would need to have the composure to get through it.

"Becky, don't worry about it. If you have to miss this for some reason, I can make up the time in the service. Please don't give it another thought."

"Thanks Russell, I plan to be there and sing, but of course we don't know how Mother's condition will progress."

By the time that we said our good-byes, I was at the hospital.

As I walk down the fourth floor hallway, I see that Laura is on the phone. She mouths to me that she is on with her husband, Bob. She has managed to find a quiet spot and she is giving him the update, both about my experience with Mom last night and the critical nature of her condition.

"Bob, honey, I just think you should come. Even if Mother pulls through this, it is a time for as many as possible to be together. Check with Chris and see if he would ride down with you. He is planning on spending Easter with us, so he may be free to travel."

Chris is the youngest of Laura's three children, just three months younger than Adrienne. He recently finished his Master's in Psychology and has been promoted in the counseling practice where he did his internship. Except for one long term relationship, he has remained single. Although he is a very handsome young man, he is serious and intense, sometimes too much for his own good. His drive and competitiveness is admirable, but that intensity can come off as inflexible and stubborn. I have told Laura over the past few years that he will temper that with age and experience, and for the most part, these are good qualities. Personally, he is one of my favorites. I certainly see the serious characteristics, but also see the vulnerability in them as well.

Laura is hanging up and indicates that Bob will drive down in the morning, hopefully with Chris. She reports that she has also spoken with Robert, her eldest, and Alicia in Colorado. Robert is standing by and will make a decision to drive down if Mother starts to decline further. Alicia has a bigger challenge. So far away, and with two small children, she will only come if Mother passes.

As Laura and I walk toward the room, I hear someone call my name and I turn to see Collette coming down the hall.

"That was quick," I said as she walked up and gave me a hug and then Laura one as well.

"I was headed here already when Russell called and said it was okay," she replied with a wink. "He always has to do the proper thing, but me, I come without permission."

"Collette, I told Russell and I will tell you too; you are always welcome. You are family." That comment instigated another hug from Collette, this one a little softer, and a little longer.

As we rounded the corner and in to Mother's room, Dad met us at the door. One look at his face told me Russell was absolutely on target; Dad was starting to get anxious. He gave me a hug and kiss, and then a huge bear hug for Collette. She smiled and hugged him back.

As I walk over to Mother, I immediately notice a change in her complexion. I don't know if Dad or Laura have spotted it yet, since they have been with her over the last few hours and the change may have been gradual, but no doubt to me, she has developed a yellow cast. I am now very worried about her kidneys. I glance at the clock and see that it is 3:30 pm. At least four more hours before Amelia is here. I need to speak with the nurse and then I need to text Amelia.

"Dad, when was the last time Mom had labs?" I ask.

"They were in here about 11:00 this morning taking some blood but I haven't heard anything since then," Dad said. He is experienced at this whole caretaker role too and despite my best nonchalant tone, he is searching my face to see what I am thinking.

"What is it honey?"

"Dad, she looks a little yellow to me. I will go talk with the nurse and see what the labs show. It has been several hours. They should have the results."

Laura moves over to Mom to look more closely and Collette puts her arm around Dad. Although it seems sometimes as if I am always hitting the panic button, the truth of the matter is that we have been through this enough to sense the smallest variations in skin, smells and demeanor (albeit Mom has only slight variations on the last one). Not ego, just fact, I am almost always right on this. You just get a sixth sense. It is kind of like the intuition you have as a mother, you just feel it; see it. I wish that sixth sense had been working yesterday morning when I was with Mother. This situation may have been better.

Oh brother, I am starting to think and sound like Dad. I try to focus on getting some answers and head down the hall looking for Holly; Mom's day nurse today.

After walking down to the other end of the fourth floor corridor, I find Holly outside another room. "Hi Holly," I greet her. "When you get a minute, I would like to get the results of the labs done on my Mother, Gloria Bridges, earlier today, room 429."

Holly indicates that she will check the labs and have the physician discuss the results with us when he completes his rounds. I know that tactic, and I am not falling for it.

"Holly, I appreciate that you want the physician to discuss these with us, but I really need to know something immediately. I have just come back to the hospital and there is no question that my Mother's complexion has a yellow cast. My concern is her kidney function, so if you could at least check her chart and give us an update that would be great."

Holly is experienced too. She, I am sure, knows how to deal with me as well. "Ms., I am sorry, I didn't catch your name . . ."

"Becky Kennedy. I am Gloria Bridges daughter."

"Yes, Ms. Kennedy. As soon as I have completed my meds round, I will check the chart and have Dr. Wilson, the floor physician on duty, come and speak with your family."

"Thank you, I really appreciate it." Not quite an 'immediate' response, but a commitment none-the-less. Sometimes you have to take what you can get. I make a mental note of the time. I need a response within the hour or I will be back with Holly.

As I walk back to Mother's room, I prepare myself. Dad will not be happy with the delay in learning the results. I send a text to Amelia with our key word; MOM. Hopefully she can prep me with the right questions to ask Dr. Wilson, when we get a chance to speak with him.

CHAPTER 9

Collette is still with Dad when I return to the room. As well, Maxine has stopped by to sit with Dad. As soon as I walk in the door, Dad wants to know if I learned anything about the labs. I indicate to him that the nurse will pull the labs and consult with the doctor. My cell phone rings and it is Amelia.

I quickly get Amelia up to speed on things. She indicates that at least for the time being, the ER at First Memorial is fairly quiet. She expects to get off on time and will come over to the hospital. I thank her and catch her up on Mom's appearance and the lack of lab information.

"Mom, it may be a symptom that the kidneys are starting to break down, but we will not know that for sure until we get the labs. As soon as you know something, text me and I will call if I can," Amelia advised.

I agreed to let her know when we had received an update. In the meantime, Dad looked like he could use a break. Maybe Maxine could convince him to get out of here and go have a real meal somewhere outside of the hospital. It is doubtful, but worth a shot.

"Dad, why don't you take Maxine over to Sam's Café and the two of you have a decent dinner. Laura, Collette and I have this for now. You need a break," I suggest in a cooperative, but encouraging tone.

Maxine gets the drift, Lord I do love her.

"Daniel, I think that is a great idea. I missed lunch and I could use the company myself," she states. Of course we all know that Maxine most likely didn't skip lunch, but she realizes that unless Dad feels like he helping someone else, he most likely will not budge.

"Okay ladies. Don't think that I am hoodwinked by your maneuvering, but I think getting out of here for a few minutes is a good idea. We will run over to Sam's since it is close by."

Fantastic! Even a little break is a big deal. We may be in for a marathon here and this is tough on him. Dad and Maxine head out and I plop down in the chair next to Collette.

"Becky," Collette says, "The ladies at the church want to do something for your family since you have Adrienne coming home and likely some of Laura's family. We will keep it simple, something that can be plated and microwaved whenever someone is at the house or feels like eating. Will Italian be okay? We are initially thinking of making lasagna, salad, bread and a vegetable casserole of some kind."

"Collette, that would be wonderful," I reply. "I know Dad would appreciate it and who knows what the next few days will bring."

"Consider it done then. We will plan to bring it over to Daniel's on Saturday afternoon. I will call you later with the details so that we can coordinate delivery."

Collette picks up her handbag and prepares to leave. Laura thanks her for everything and we both promise to stay in touch and keep her and Russell posted on Mother's condition.

Finally, it is just Laura and I again and nothing yet from Holly or the doctor. I reach down to check my telephone and see a message from Adrienne. She is requesting some input on what she should pack in preparation for the weekend; given Mother's hospitalization. Our plan prior to Mother's medical emergency had been to hang out by the pool and take long walks on the beach. The only structured plan we had was a final fitting on her bridesmaid dress at Wedding

Royale, the bridal shop where we purchased both Amelia's and the bridesmaid dresses. I text her back and suggest that in addition to her bathing suit and shorts, she may want to bring a sweater and some jeans to deal with the air conditioning in the hospital.

I glance up and see Laura dozing in the chair. She has been here a long time and needs to go back to Dad's house and get some rest. Maybe when Amelia gets here, I can convince her to do that.

I quietly scoot my chair up next to Mother and place my hand on top of her arm, the sheet separating our touch. She doesn't move or respond. I continue to hold her and begin humming quietly the song that I am supposed to sing on Sunday at Church. The hum transitions to words and I sing quietly.

"I can only imagine, what it will be like, when I . . ."

This is such a beautiful song and given the experience with Mother last night, I really hope that I will be able to sing it on Sunday. What a beautiful tribute to our Heavenly Father on Easter Sunday.

Laura stirs from her nap as I finish the song. "That was beautiful," she said.

"I am sorry if I disturbed you. I just know it comforts Mother when I sing to her, and to tell you the truth, it comforts me too."

"I loved it. Your singing will never disturb me," Laura replied.

"Name a tune then, and we will sing to her together."

Just as Laura looked like she was going to suggest one, Dr. Wilson came in the room, followed by Holly.

"Hello, I am Dr. Wilson, the staff physician on fourth floor today."

"Hi Dr. Wilson, it is nice to meet you. I am Becky Kennedy and this is Laura Cox. We are Gloria Bridges daughters."

Dr. Wilson walked over to Mother's bed and greeted her by name. He picked up her hand and called her by name again. Mother opened her eyes just enough to see through the slits in the bottom and closed her eyes again.

"Has she responded to any of you today?" he asked. I shook my head at the same time that I responded verbally.

"We have just noticed today that her skin is tinted yellow and we have concerns for jaundice," I said. Dr. Wilson looked at the chart again and then addressed us.

"Her red blood count is elevated, showing a higher than usual amount of bilirubin. This most likely is the onset of jaundice symptoms. I am not yet certain why this situation may be occurring but it could be several things. Since her bacterial infection is still present, this may have caused inflammation of the bladder or liver. She may also have developed some type of block in the intestine. This is unlikely but at this point we are not ruling out any potential causes. I have reviewed her medication and I do not believe she has been taking any meds that would create this symptomology. Right now, we will treat her as if it is a by-product of the original infection. If we can clear the infection, this will most likely clear as well."

I thank Dr. Wilson and call Amelia's cell phone. She is satisfied for the time being with the doctor's conclusions and indicates she will be leaving work shortly and will see us soon.

Dad returns without Maxine, having seen her to her car prior to heading up to the hospital room. Laura and I update him on the doctor's visit and Amelia's comments supporting the doctor's plan. Dad seems a little more relaxed and seems to feel better about Mom's condition being addressed.

A few minutes later a lab tech came in the room for more blood and urine samples. She indicated that the doctor just ordered these and has placed a 'stat' request. This is good. It is an indication that he is taking the situation seriously and is looking for any significant change since the lab work earlier in the day.

Amelia rings my cell phone to indicate that she is on the way. She offers to stop and get take-out for Laura and I. We order sandwiches and I end the call. Laura needs to go home and get some rest. Hopefully, when Amelia gets here, I can convince her to do that.

I sit next to Dad and hold his hand. We begin talking about Adrienne's visit, Chris and Bob's drive down tomorrow, and the status of his other grandchildren. We don't make any plans. We know from experience, this is a wait and see deal.

CHAPTER 10

Amelia arrives at the hospital around 7:00 pm with sandwiches, chips and diet sodas for Laura and me. As soon as she sets the food down, she heads over to Mother's bedside.

"Grandma, it is me, Amelia. Can you open your eyes and look at me?" Amelia leans over the bed and folds the sheet back to examine Mother's skin. She checks her legs and removes her hospital socks to look at her feet and toes. She raises Mother's hospital gown to check the skin on the torso.

"I wish I could get her to open her eyes," Amelia said. She raises Mother's eyelid to see if she can get a look at the color on the whites of mother's eyes. "Grandma, it is Amelia. I want you to wake up and look at me. You know I am getting married in two short months. Pretty soon, I will be Amelia Temple, instead of Amelia Kennedy. I am very excited, Grandma."

Mother's sleep is deep and Amelia gets no response. Tears well up in my eyes and I know that I am either going to stand there and cry, or get busy. I choose the latter. Crying seems like a bad idea. I head over to the end of the bed and begin to straighten Mother's bed sheets. I rub Mother's feet, hoping to create some sort of response for Amelia. As I rub Mother's feet, I feel her gently stretching her toes. I comment on that to Amelia.

Dad looks at Amelia expectantly. "Amelia honey, what do you think?" Dad inquires.

Amelia knows better than try to bluff with her Grandfather. "Granddad, I believe she has a pretty high fever and her sepsis is still present, although it is definitely better than it was when she was admitted yesterday. There are some symptoms of jaundice and that could be from several things. The combination of the two indicates some struggle going on in her system. We will see what the last labs say, and just keep an eye on her," Amelia advised. After checking the IV bags, Amelia confirmed that Mother is being treated with a strong antibiotic and is also receiving fluids to avoid dehydration and to produce urine. Urine output will be important as part of the diagnostic information, especially if kidney issues are suspected.

Dad seemed satisfied that Amelia was 'on the job' and shooting straight with him on Mother's condition. I took that opportunity to encourage Dad and Laura to go home and get some rest.

"Dad, Laura, both of you should go home and get some rest. We have a long night tonight and a big day tomorrow. Adrienne is coming in, as is Bob and hopefully Chris. You both want to be rested and ready to enjoy your time with them."

Dad picked up his sunglasses and cap from the bedside table without any objections to the idea of going home and getting rest. "Laura, you know better than to argue with your sister. Let's leave these two girls alone and head home."

Laura looked hesitant but knew in our shared glance that her job wasn't over. Someone needed to be with Dad. "You got it Dad. I could use a recliner and a cup of hot tea. This has been a long day."

By the time we got them out of the room it was 8:00 pm. As Amelia sat down in one of the chairs on the opposite side of Mother's bed, she gave me a direct look. I knew she was going to share her real concerns about Mother.

"Mom, this is not good. Either sepsis or jaundice at Grandma's age are symptoms of a much bigger problem. Both together is critical. The fever and seizure activity on top of both of these is a lot for her to overcome in her condition."

"Amelia, what are you saying? Are you suggesting that perhaps we should begin to prepare the rest of the family for the significance of this?" Amelia knew as well as I did that we have had many scares in the past where Mother pulled through with amazing recovery.

"Mom, I don't see how this can end well. I know we have had these situations before, but this is really not good."

I suggest that we wait until the morning and see what her condition is at that time. It is already getting late and tomorrow is Good Friday. Both she and Adrienne will be here. Hopefully Chris will travel with Bob, so the other family that would need to be considered is Robert and Alicia. Since both of those are Laura's children, she will have to make that call on whether to instruct them on Mother's condition. Amelia and I sit quietly for a few moments.

"Mom, I am supposed to be off tomorrow but Leslie has agreed to switch with me so that I can have Easter Sunday off with the family. I am grateful to her because I would really like to have the extra time with Adrienne and of course I would like to be with the family, especially with Grandma's condition.

"Amelia, that would be great," I replied.

Just as I was finishing my sentence, Amelia's cell phone vibrated.

"It is Craig", she says as she begins to text him back. "He just landed at the airport and is headed to his condo. I will give him a call in a few minutes and give him an update. He wants to know if I want him to come down to the hospital."

"Amelia, you need to go home tonight and get some rest. I will be fine here with Mother. You are scheduled to work tomorrow and by the time you get off, I will be back from the airport with Adrienne."

"I can stay for a while Mother. I want to be here with you and Grandma."

She is truly a chip off of the old block. I refrain from pushing her on going home, since I completely understand the need to be here.

She and I talked about her shift at the hospital. She had a case early in the day of a teen bitten by a shark on the leg. The young man will be fine, but her interactions with the family had been exhausting. Apparently the Mom and Dad are divorced and they had a fight in the lobby on whose fault the shark bite was and threats on repercussion.

"*Really*", Amelia said. "Your child has been bitten by a shark in the ocean and you want to blame each other? Get with the program and count your blessings that 30 stitches and a story to tell are the only issues you are leaving the hospital with."

Amelia ran through a few other cases and then updated a regular litany that she has on one of the ER doctors; Brad Knight. Today Brad's offensive behavior was his treatment of one of the nurse aides. Apparently she didn't jump quite high enough when he asked her to retrieve some sterile tools and he berated her in front of the patient and the patient's family. As Amelia recounted that story, I thought steam would come through her ears.

We continued to chat about her day, when all of a sudden Mother opened her eyes. As I stepped over to the bed, she raised one of her hands slightly off of the bed and turned her head to the left.

"Mom, hi, how are you feeling?" Mom stared through me, a response that I am accustomed to. It is how I best explain that vacant stare of a long term Alzheimer patient.

"Hi Grandma, its Amelia", Amelia said, reaching out to hold Mother's hand. "Did you have a good sleep?"

I grab one of the flavored aloe swabs from the bedside stand and begin to swab her lips. She sucks slightly on the swab, the most response that I have had since her hospitalization. I continue chit chat, talking about the family and general stuff. She is awake and looking around the room within her face-forward field of vision.

In the nursing home, we have things hanging on strings over the bed so that she has things to look at when she is awake. I wonder for a moment if she misses those things, if maybe she realizes that she is not in her room, her familiar surroundings. Logic would deny that, since Mother's memory even 5 or 6 years ago was so poor she could not remember things that occurred just minutes before, but I will be the first to admit that we do not know what registers in the brain with those who have Alzheimer's.

Amelia is holding her right hand and I reach out for her left hand. I begin to sing to her quietly and Amelia joins in the song. We are singing "Morning Has Broken" in beautiful harmony. Mom's grip on my hand is firm and she continues the constant pressure. These hands have been her voice for so many years. She conveys through her touch the most basic communication; comfort and peace.

We sit together, the three of us, and I am so grateful that Amelia has had this experience. Her grandmother has been sick for so much of her life, yet Amelia is so close to her. No doubt, the inability to help her grandmother is one of the reasons Amelia has said that she went to medical school. My mother has been an ever-present on the job training for all of us. I say a quiet prayer, for my daughter, my mother, and I lift up my spirit for God's refreshment. I am blessed and so grateful.

I reach over and kiss my mother on the cheek. I tell her I love her, and we sit with her until her eyes close and she is lost again in her world of sleep. I look over at Amelia and see tears streaming down her face. I understand the heartbreak of loss, and so does she. Are we on the edge of losing my Mother, her Grandmother? We have no way of knowing.

GOOD FRIDAY

Chapter 11

I am startled awake by one of the night nurse aides in the room checking Mother's vitals. I look at my watch and realize that I must have actually slept a couple of hours.

After I was able to convince Amelia to go home and get some rest, I had prayed over Mother and then settled myself in to a chaise lounge recliner that one of the nurses had moved to the room, since it was apparent to them that someone from the family would be staying around the clock with Mother.

I walk over to Mother's bed and notice that she is wide awake. Her eyes are clear, although always vacant, and she looks like herself. I reach to pull the string on the overhead light above the bed to get a better look at her. The whites of her eyes do not show any trace of yellow and her skin tone looks better.

"Mother looks better right now than she has looked since she arrived here," I remark to the nurse. "How were the latest labs? Is her infection subsiding?"

"Her last labs showed some improvement in both the level of infection and the level of bilirubin in the blood. I would say she has improved some but it is early and these things have a way of going up and down."

I looked at her name tag; Janet. "Janet, when will the next labs be taken?"

Janet indicates that the next set of labs is to be taken at 7:00 am. I looked at my watch again noting that it is 3:00 am.

"What is her temperature?" I asked as she completed the vitals. "She has a low grade fever, just below one hundred degrees. Her blood pressure is back within normal range at 140/88."

I marvel at the resilience of my Mother. So many times she has been at the brink of death and has managed to come through. It is truly amazing and confirms what we already know; God, not us, decides when it is our time to leave this earth. I coach myself on not getting my hopes up, but clearly this is a good sign.

After Janet leaves, I reach over and hold Mother's hands. "Mother, it is nice to have you back. You have been pretty sick, but it looks like you are on the mend. I am so happy Mom. Dad will be thrilled when he gets up here in a little bit. We love you so much."

Her distance is in her mind, but I believe in my heart that she feels comfort in our touch and our expressions of love.

After sitting with Mother for a while, I get up to stretch and walk down the hall and back a few times. I notice as I pass other rooms that most of the patients are in their rooms without family. I know people probably think we are unusual, but honestly, I can't imagine leaving my Mother in critical condition; unable to ring a call bell or express her discomfort. I would not want to be anywhere else but here, with her.

On my way back to the room Janet stops me to offer a cup of coffee. I could easily go down to the cafeteria, but that would be coffee out of a machine. I gratefully accept, even without her convincing me that the pot is freshly brewed.

I sit down on the end of Mother's bed and sip my coffee, watching her rest. Her eyes are closed again, but her face looks peaceful. I pull back the sheet to look at her skin, checking to see if the red blotches from the sepsis are better, and clearly there is improvement.

As I sit with her, I reflect back to earlier times in this horrific disease. Each stage has been difficult, but probably the most difficult were the early stages. I remember how hard it was to accept this illness and frankly how little we knew about Alzheimer's twenty years ago.

As a family, the decision to take her keys so that she couldn't drive her car anymore was heart-wrenching. She was so angry, which was an emotion that we had really never seen from her. She lashed out at all of us, but Dad really took the harshest wrath from her. I remember her accusations as if they happened yesterday. Although we knew that she was no longer safe to drive, for her own safety as well as others, it was still so difficult to see her anguish over losing that independence.

As I recalled the stages that led us to this point, each progression had challenges that were unforeseen and so difficult to manage. Probably the worst for Dad was the celebration of their fiftieth wedding anniversary. Laura and I had coordinated a dinner in their honor at a local restaurant and family and friends were invited to the celebration. Mom looked amazing in a knee-length gold lame dress with an ivory lace jacket and ivory silk pumps. She visited with everyone during the evening and she and Dad had a great time. When Dad woke up the next morning and reminisced about the great evening, Mother had no recollection and accused him of fabricating the story. What a sad day for him and for all of us as we realized the degree of memory loss that she suffered and what seemed to be a fast decline compared to earlier stages.

Of course, that was ten years ago and at that time I would not have believed that she would decline to the point that she had just two years later, when she began to not recognize her family and close friends. Shortly after, she suffered two strokes and I never heard her speak again. The musical voice was gone forever.

It has been over seven years since she has spoken my name and longer than that since she has recognized me as her youngest daughter. A single tear slips down my cheek as my eyes begin to brim with tears. I intentionally exit the memories and force myself in to the present. I can't be emotional right now. If I am, I fear I won't be able to stop the flood that surely will follow. Conjuring up memories of this brain-robbing disease is too difficult.

I settle in the chair next to Mother's bed and open my Bible. I keep a list of favorite scripture in the note pages and I began reading them. Over the last few years, these scriptures have been the light in my darkness, the calm in my grief, the comfort in my calamity as I coped with Roger's unexpected death.

Hebrews 11:1;

"Now faith is being sure of what we hope for and certain of what we do not see."

Funny, I think, but I am sure that I have seen hope; in my Mother's brief exchange night before last with the other side, and in my own life as I have felt God literally wrap his arms around me in the days and weeks following Roger's passing. One thing is for sure, no one can convince me that the Spirit of our Holy God is not living in each of us that believes in Him and seeks Him.

One of the scriptures I have relied on most over the past few years; Proverbs 3:5;

"Trust in the Lord with all of your heart and lean not on your own understanding."

The last twenty years of my life has been reliant on this very verse. Coping with the reality of a Mother who doesn't recognize you results in a level of sadness beyond understanding. And when a Mother is as terrific as mine, you wonder how this can happen. How can a mother not remember that we cooked dinner, when we are in the middle of cleaning the kitchen after dinner? How can a mother not remember that her own child has her own children? How can a Mother who is sixty years old not have the memory to tell the manager of a grocery store where she lives, when she is sitting on the curb in front of the store crying and confused?

Lord, I have trusted you, I think to myself. *If I didn't have my faith, I could not have coped with any of it.*

I move on to the next comfort scripture, James 1:2-3.

"Consider it pure joy, my brothers, whenever you face trials of many kinds, because you know that the testing of your faith develops perseverance."

Wow, I have pondered on that one many hours. But as I reflect, I know that in my heart of hearts, I believe this. I believe that when we follow Him, God prepares us to do His will, and teaches us through life experiences to best handle and cope with the challenges we face.

"Thank you Lord," I pray quietly. "You have delivered us all from evil and have shed Your light on our lives and blessed them in so many ways. Thank you for every day that I have spent loving You and thank you for my amazing earthly family. Amen."

"And Amen," said my earthly father.

"Dad, I didn't hear you come in," I said as I glanced at my watch. It was 4:30 am. "I am so glad you are here. Did you get some rest?"

"I did. And, I think your sister did too. I peeked in on her before I left and she was sound asleep. I didn't want to wake her."

"Mom is better Dad. Her fever is down, the jaundice is going away and her blood work is better. I was just thanking God for pulling us through this. The nurse did caution me that this could be a swing in her condition and not a clear indication of improvement, but I am the forever optimist. Mom was awake for a while. I was able to spend some time with her."

Dad looks so relieved. Bless his heart, he loves her so much. He sits down on the bed and holds her hand.

"Gloria, wake up honey. I want to say good morning."

Mom opened her eyes and you could see her attempt a smile. Although she hasn't spoken since my girls were in their late teens, early twenties, she knows the sound of my father's voice.

"Good morning beautiful," my father croons. "You are a sleepy head this morning."

Dad smiles as he holds her hand and gives her a kiss on her cheek. He smoothes her hair back from her forehead and plants a kiss there. He continues to talk to her and begins to tell her about the day ahead. Adrienne, her granddaughter is coming home for the weekend. Bob, Laura and Chris are coming for Easter weekend.

I listen to him talk to her as if she understands everything he is saying. The lift in his tone and his focus on normalcy is a daily routine for him and he always includes her. I feel tears at the corners of my eye and excuse myself to the restroom. Although I love his devotion to her, I am too emotional to watch it. I know my emotions stem from several things; knowing we will lose her someday soon, knowing that my father will be devastated, and mostly knowing that I will likely never have that relationship with someone. My Roger would have been an anchor in a stormy sea, and although not at all like my Father in most ways, he would have taken care of me with love and devotion. That history is gone. That future is gone.

As I wash my hands in the restroom, I catch a glimpse of myself. I am tired, but I also see sadness in those eyes. A sadness for what has been, and what will be. My scripture comes back to comfort me; Psalm 28:7;

"The Lord is my strength and my shield, my heart trusts in Him and I am helped."

As I round the corner into Mother's room, I see Dad packing my things. He looks at me and tells me it is time that I go get some rest. I will go to his house and sleep in his other guest room. For once, I don't argue. I believe that he will cherish time with my mother alone, Mother is doing better, and I am tired and weary.

As I make my way down the hall, I think of my own daughter coming home today. It will be so wonderful to see her, to hold her in my arms, and to be close to her for a few days.

CHAPTER 12

I am rested and getting ready to leave for the airport when I hear a car in the drive at Dad's house. I look out the window to see Bob and Chris getting out of their car. I open the front door and catch Bob in a huge hug.

"Bob, Chris it is so great to see you! You are earlier than I thought you would be, Laura is going to be thrilled to see you."

"I just spoke to her a few minutes ago. She said that she would meet us here. She should be here anytime," Bob said. "How are you holding up Becky? I know this has been a long couple of days for you."

"Bob, I am doing well, better now that both of you are here. I will be doing even better when I pick up Adrienne in a little while. Chris, I know Amelia and Adrienne are going to be so happy to see you."

"I can't wait to see them too, Aunt Becky. I haven't even met Amelia's fiancé and she is almost married."

"Yeah," Bob chimed in. "What are we going to do if he doesn't meet mine and Chris' approval? Amelia really should have taken that in to consideration before agreeing to spend the rest of her life with this guy," Bob teased.

"Bob, make sure you tell her that when you see her later, she definitely needs both of your approvals before the "I do's" happen."

We all laugh. Partly at the fun, but mostly realizing that Amelia is one strong personality and we know that our opinion is desired but not necessarily heeded.

Laura arrives while we are standing in the driveway. She looks beautiful today, in navy twill pants and a pressed navy and white striped button-down shirt. She has navy espadrilles to complete the outfit, along with a navy and gold tone belt with a designer logo on a charm hanging off the buckle. Her diamond hoop earrings frame her face and her hair is stylishly done.

Bob walks over to her and gives her a hug and a kiss. Chris follows his father and gives his Mom a hug. Chris and Bob both tower over Laura. Laura, at five feet six inches tall is several inches shorter than I am and the 'short one' of the family.

Laura assures me that Mother has continued to improve, so I feel much better about being away from the hospital. I notice the time and tell them that I need to leave to get Adrienne. They will go see Mom, taking both Bob's car and Dad's truck so that Dad has his own transportation at the hospital. I promise them that Adrienne and I will come to the hospital once I pick her up at the airport. I hope that we can all go to dinner together later, and really hope we can convince Dad to come. I will text Amelia and see if she and Craig will be able to join us.

As I drive to the airport, I call Pastor Russell James. I need to let him know that Mother is doing better and hopefully I will be able to sing the solo in church on Sunday. I get Russell's voice mail and leave him a message.

As I end my call, the phone rings. It is Amelia checking to see if I am on the way to pick up Adrienne. I let her know that I am and Amelia indicates that she may be late getting off today. There has been a boating accident on the bay and two rescue trucks are on their way to the ER where she is on duty. Depending on the seriousness of the injuries, she may be held over for a while.

"Amelia that is fine. Chris and Bob just arrived and they are going over to the hospital to sit with Mom and Dad. Adrienne's flight is scheduled to arrive at 4:30 and she and I will head over to the hospital from there. I am hoping that we can all have dinner later, maybe at Captain Harry's, out on the deck." It would be a beautiful evening to sit out on the waterfront and have some good seafood.

"That will work great for us if I can get off at a reasonable hour. 7:00 o'clock would probably work, but I have to go now, the rescue trucks are within the block. Love you Mom."

As Amelia hung up, I said a quiet prayer for those injured in the boating accident. They are in good hands with Amelia and the rest of the ER team.

As I park the car in the airport garage and make my way to the terminal, I catch myself with a big smile. I truly cannot wait to see Adrienne. She should be landing in the next fifteen minutes or so. My spirits lift at the thought of seeing my youngest.

69

Chapter 13

Adrienne is scheduled to come in on U.S. Airways from Charlotte and I quickly scan the flight status on the board as I enter the main concourse area where non-ticketed individuals can wait for arriving passengers. Adrienne's flight number is blinking with "Arrived" as the status. Wow—she is early. I hope I haven't missed her exit the gate area. I look around and as I turn back to the main waiting area, I see her coming toward me. She is grinning and waving—what a thrill!

"Adrienne, you look stunning! Stand back and let me take a look at you." As she complies she grabs her hair self-consciously and tucks her chin a bit. My exuberance, although truly appreciated by her, is also a little too much public display and I recognize her discomfort. As I reach for another hug, we turn in the direction of baggage claim. Her tall, thin frame is in stylish skinny jeans with a black turtle neck sweater and a brown leather motorcycle styled jacket. Her boots are a riding boot style in brown and black leather. She could model for any magazine.

"Mom, tell me about Grandma. I have had such a hard time today trying to get work done with her on my mind."

"Well, honey, most of today she has been better. Last night when I stayed with her she had some moments of being alert and when your grandfather came in early this morning to relieve me, she actually gave him a smile. Of course, she isn't out of the woods yet, but I know your grandfather will be so happy you are here."

"I can't wait to see him Mom. We are going to the hospital first, right?"

"Absolutely. We will see your grandparents and you also get to see Chris, Aunt Laura and Uncle Bob. They are all here now."

"That is great! I can't wait to see Chris, it has been so long. I also want to see Amelia and hear about the rest of the wedding plans. I can't believe she is getting married in June."

As we walk to the car, I give Adrienne more details on her grandmother, the doctor reports, and the close calls. As I chat, I can't help but swell with adoration for this daughter of mine. Her concern for her grandmother is so sincere, and her love for both her grandparents such a part of her fiber. Although living away from us, it is clear from her end of the conversation that we are part of her daily thoughts and prayers.

As we drive out of the airport, Adrienne becomes silent and thoughtful, looking out the window and stroking her arm.

"Adrienne, is everything okay?"

"Yes, everything is fine Mom. I am just thinking about how I would feel if something happened to Grandma while I was gone. It just hit me as we started driving that it would hurt to be away and not be here for you and Granddad if she passed away."

Adrienne's sincerity is authentic. She is so serious and always so responsible. "Honey, we understand that you can't be here all the time. I don't want you to feel guilty or feel like you are letting us down."

"Mom, I know what you are saying, but the distance would be awful. When Dad died, one of the things that I remember most was all of us together, loving and supporting each other. It would be hard to be away."

And at this moment I realize, although she would feel bad for us, her real hurt would be in her aloneness before she could reach us. I feel my heart going out to her and know that this sensitive, beautiful young woman needs us in ways that sometimes we forget in the shadow of independence, successful careers, and the growing up of our children. I put my hand on her hand and our eyes meet.

"Sweetheart, if you are away when something happens to your grandmother, your Heavenly Father's arms are around you and us, and we will be together as soon as we can. I will need you and you will need all of us."

As I finish, I can feel a tear in the corner of my eye. As I let go of her hand to wipe my tear, I notice that she is doing the same. We look at each other and start laughing.

"Mom, you made me cry and that is the last thing I want to do is be all soppy *before* I see Grandma and Granddad. Can we stop and get a coffee or something? Regroup and collect ourselves?"

"That sounds like an excellent idea. We are only a few miles from the hospital. Let's get a tray of coffee in case others want some. Hopefully we are all going to be meeting at Captain Harry's around 7:00 for dinner."

As we pull in to grab coffees, Adrienne sheds her jacket in the Florida cool night, milder than the Charlotte cold that she has just left. She looks so chic—one of those girls that manages to be chic and unassuming at the same time.

As we drive the rest of the way to the hospital, Adrienne fills me in on some of her projects at work and new responsibilities that she has been given in the last week; a clear sign of her continued development and value to the software company where she works as a staff attorney.

As she talks, part of me keeps returning to our discussion about her being away if something happened to her grandmother. Something doesn't feel right. Mother's intuition or whatever, more is going on with Adrienne. I make a mental note to better understand what if anything is on her mind while she is home for the weekend.

About a mile from the hospital, my cell rings. As I reach for the phone, I tease with Adrienne about the family pack being impatient for her to arrive. As we both laugh, my smile quickly disappears when I see the caller ID. Matthew Green. Matthew is one of the attorneys in town who has recently made it clear to me that he is interested in a personal relationship.

Not tonight—I am not talking to him tonight. I silence the ring and put the phone back in my purse, but not before Adrienne's suspicion surfaces. Adrienne grabs the phone out of my bag and hits 'recent calls'.

"Okay Mom, who is Matthew Green?" Adrienne pried. "And don't tell me he is a client because I saw your face a minute ago and that is not how you look when one of your client's call."

"No, that is another attorney in town. He and I are working on a common case and I am not in the mood to talk to him about it right now." It was mostly true, I do have a real estate foreclosure client that was also represented by Matthew for some other legal issues.

"Not buying it Mom. You had an instant of pure fear in your face. If I had to guess, he has the make on you and you are running for your life." As Adrienne hit the nail on the head, she knew that too. She slapped her leg and started laughing. "Mom, you are blushing! This must be a really good story. I am going to get the low down from Amelia. She knows everything."

"Well, she doesn't know this. I have been avoiding Matthew's advances for the past month. I don't know why he is so persistent. I haven't been very accommodating to his suggestions for getting together. He is not my type and I don't have any time anyway," I admitted.

The truth is I don't want to date. I wish I wanted to date, but I don't. It would be nice to have someone to go to dinner with, maybe a play or a sporting event, but I draw the line at intimacy. In my wildest dreams, I don't see myself intimate with another man. Maybe more time . . . maybe.

"Mom, you are hot! Are you kidding me? Of course he is after you. Who wouldn't be, that is the better question?"

As I look at Adrienne, she is being playful. I wonder how she would really feel if I were to get intimate with someone other than her father. Who knows, maybe I am the one stuck in the past.

Chris and Bob are standing outside the hospital when we pull in to the parking lot. Adrienne sees Chris and rolls down the window with a wave. Her grin transforms into a look of concern as she gets a closer look at their expressions.

"Mom, something is wrong. Oh no!" and with that Adrienne is out of the car with me close behind her.

Bob was the first to reach out to Adrienne and give her a hug and kiss, followed by Chris. As Bob hugged Adrienne, his face over her shoulder met mine. Adrienne pulled back from the hugs just as I asked the question, "Bob, what is going on?"

"Your Mother was doing pretty well until about a half hour ago. All of a sudden her blood pressure spiked pretty well and things have gone downhill from there. You better go ahead and see Laura and your Dad. I know they are waiting for you. We didn't call, figured you would be here any minute."

As Adrienne and I hurry to the elevator, my heart is racing. I check my watch and see that it is almost 5:45. I wonder if anyone has called Amelia. I start to dial her and remember that she was in the middle of a large emergency when I spoke with her last. I will wait until I know more and then call her.

Bob and Chris remained downstairs and so Adrienne and I enter the room. One look at mother and I am shocked. She is pale, and the left side of her face seems to be drooping.

"Dad, I just spoke to Bob downstairs, what happened?" He is clearly upset and asks Laura to fill me in. He puts his arms around Adrienne and tells her he loves her. The two of them sit down on two of the chairs in the room, Adrienne's attention focused on her Aunt Laura.

"Well," Laura started, "things were going pretty well. There were times today when she was awake and seemed somewhat alert and other times when she was sleeping peacefully. About 5:00 she had what seemed like small seizures and alarms started going off. The nurses and doctor came in and gave her some more of that anti-seizure medicine but it didn't stop. They gave her something else and she seemed to calm down. Her blood pressure was over 200 and the doctor basically said we are back to touch and go."

"Has anyone spoken with Amelia?" I asked.

"No, we wanted to wait until you got here," Dad said.

"Who is the nurse assigned to Mother this afternoon?" I asked.

"There are several but I think the main one is Holly," Dad said.

Great, I thought sarcastically. This could be a tough road to get any good information. I decide to call Amelia and see what time she is going to get off. Hopefully she can come by here and talk with the personnel on duty before their shift is up.

Amelia answers on the third ring. "Hi Mom, did you get Adrienne?" I explained that Adrienne and I are at the hospital and as much as I know on Mom's condition.

"What time do you think you will be off?" I asked.

"Mom, I should be able to leave shortly. I am finishing up the paperwork but my shift relief is already here. I can be out of here in maybe twenty minutes; there in forty-five."

"Perfect. The sooner the better."

As I round the corner to go back in to mother's room, the alarms are sounding again. Adrienne and Dad both rush to mother's bed and Laura turns on the light over the bed. Holly and the staff physician are right behind me as I enter the room.

After examining mother and checking the medication drips, Dr. Wilson asks us if we have contacted Hospice. We indicate that we have not and he encourages us to consider contacting Hospice soon. He also asks if we would like to speak to clergy and we reply that our pastor is a close family friend and we can call him at any time.

I ask Dr. Wilson mother's current status and what he thinks we are looking at in the way of her prognosis.

"I think your mother is losing the fight with the infection. Based on her stat labs that we had done an hour or so ago, we believe that her general system is beginning to respond to the prolonged infection and it is likely that we will continue to see her physiological breakdown. The seizure-like episodes are likely spasmodic responses to her kidneys shutting down and the sepsis state of her blood. We are giving her heavy doses of antibiotics and although we thought we had early signs of progress, those signs are no longer evident. We will see what the next twenty-four hours bring, but I think you should prepare the family. Can I answer any questions for you?" asked Dr. Wilson.

"Not right now," stated Dad. "My granddaughter will be here in a little while and she may have some questions."

With a nod, Dr. Wilson and Holly leave the room. Adrienne's tears are running down her face and she has pulled out a handful of Kleenex. Laura wraps her arms around my father as Bob and Chris step back in the room, overhearing the doctor's prognosis from the doorway.

"I will be back in a minute. I am going to call Pastor James. Hopefully he and Collette can come down to the hospital," I said.

As I walked out of the room, Adrienne followed. I turn to put my arms around her. We hold each other in the hallway as she silently cries and I blink back my own tears. Mentally I am not giving up yet. It is all so sudden.

"Mom," Adrienne cried, "I can't believe that we may be losing Grandma. I didn't get a chance to say good-bye to her."

"Adrienne, you will get to say good-bye to your grandmother. Even if she doesn't understand you, her spirit will know that you are there. Let's call Pastor James. I know he will want to be here."

CHAPTER 14

I called Pastor James and Collette to let them know that we needed their prayers for my Mother and our family. Pastor James was just leaving to visit a family whose daughter had been diagnosed with Stage 4 cancer. He indicated that he would be by the hospital when his visit was completed. Collette apparently could not get to her car fast enough, as she was on the way by the time I hung up with Russell.

I then put in a call to Hospice, using the number provided by Holly. The after-hours receptionist indicated that she would have the nurse on call, Anne Rogers, ring my cell phone as soon as she was available. I hadn't had much experience with Hospice but I had met the director of the local branch during a real estate transaction for their new building. John Stillman had been courteous and reliable in my conversations with him. As I remembered his name, I recalled how much I had admired his commitment to Hospice and this community.

As I walk back to Mother's room, the finality of the situation with the call to Hospice hits me hard in the gut. For a moment I just stop in the hallway and brace myself against the wall. I fight back the tears that want to come. I need to be strong right now. There will be time for all of the emotion later. I remind myself that only God knows His plan and until He takes our Mother home with Him, she is still here with us and my family needs me.

As I regain my composure, I start to pray silently. *"Heavenly Father, be with us, surround us with your love and comfort. Hold my*

Mother in your arms gently and when you deem her time, welcome her in heaven with all of the angels singing. In your Holy Name I pray."

Looking up and standing up, I see Collette just a few feet in front of me. She had stopped to allow me to finish my prayer, but now came forward in a rush to put her arms around me. The tears that I had fought off began to roll and I could not stop crying. Her arms engulfed me and her warmth surrounded me.

"Becky, I am so sorry. Russell and I are here for you," she said as she released me. She put her arm through mine and guided me away from Mother's room and in the direction of the restroom.

While she waited, I rinsed my face and blew my nose. Looking in the mirror I realized that there wasn't much I could do. My eyes were red, my face shiny from the rinse-off of the make-up and the lines around my face seemed like large crevices compared to just a few hours ago when I was getting ready to pick up Adrienne. Oh well, it's not about me.

"Collette thank you for coming. It means so much to me and I know it will be so helpful to the rest of the family," I said as we left the restroom.

As we neared Mother's room, Amelia and Craig were coming down the hall. After giving Amelia and Craig a hug, Amelia said that Dad was worried about me and had requested she and Craig look for me.

"Mom, he needs you. He knows that you went to call the pastor, and probably Hospice, but he thinks you have been gone too long. Are you okay?" Amelia asked.

"I am okay honey. I have been able to speak with Hospice and they are going to have the nurse on duty contact us as soon as she is available. Craig it is good to see you. I hate that you have had to fly in to this situation but we love you and are grateful that you are here."

"I am glad to be here, Mrs. Kennedy. I wish I could have been here earlier but I am here now," he said as he tightened his arm around Amelia.

We begin walking in the direction of Mother's room. As we approach, I can hear Dad talking to someone in his 'authority' voice, which is usually reserved for newcomers and those he wants to be authoritative to.

"Here is my daughter Becky now," he tells the woman in the room.

I reach out my hand to introduce myself. "Hi, I am Becky Kennedy, Gloria and Dan Bridges daughter."

"Hello, I am Anne Rogers from Hospice. I was in the hospital with another patient when I received the message to contact you so I thought I would stop by in person."

"That is wonderful, thank you very much. Dad, have you been able to fill Anne in on Mom's condition?"

"We had just started. Laura and I were going over the details of the last few days. Adrienne, Chris and Bob went down to make calls to Robert and Alicia." Dad turned to Anne and explained the other family members who are here and those who may decide to travel given Mother's condition. Dad also introduced Collette to Anne.

Anne began to explain Hospice's role over the next days or weeks. As she spoke, it occurred to me how valuable this service is, but especially how much it must mean to people who do not have the support system that we have in our family. I thought of all of the hospital room doors I had looked in over the last thirty six hours and how many of those did not have any family or visitors.

My mind began to wander as she spoke, thinking about all of the older adults living in Florida who have no immediate family in the area. The 'snowbirds' as they are commonly referred to, and how lonely it must be for them.

I catch myself in the midst of my thoughts and focus again on Anne. She has asked if we have any questions and I realize that I have completely tuned her out and missed much of what she said.

No one had any questions and so we thanked her for coming and promised to call her beeper if there was any immediate change in Mother. She also left behind some basic information on Hospice. Thank goodness, because I would need to read it later.

"Becky, Laura," Dad summoned, "let's step outside. I want to talk to the two of you for a minute."

As we complied, I saw Amelia and Craig exchange a look. It symbolized I think what we were all feeling; a sense of dread and an overwhelming sadness. We walked down to the small waiting room at the end of the hall, which thankfully was empty.

"Girls, we need to think about the next few hours and what to do about our family and their needs."

"What did you have in mind?" I asked.

"Well, we have most of the family here and probably at least Robert on the way. This could be a few hours or a few weeks, we don't know. I need all of you to be available and ready should your Mother's condition change, but I also want you to try and spend time with each other. It is what your Mother would want and it is what I want. Becky, you have a daughter getting married in a few weeks. I am sure there is something to do while these two sisters are here together to get ready for this wedding. Laura, this is a time that you and your family could use to get to know Craig and be supportive to Amelia in this important and happy time in her life."

"Dad, I hear what you are saying, but this is a difficult time. My girls want to be with their grandmother. I want to be with my Mother. I think we need to let things happen naturally. I promise, we will not spend all of the time at the hospital, but right now, this is where everyone wants to be," I rationalized.

"Dad," Laura spoke up, "let us have some time with Mom now that her condition has worsened and then we will come up with a plan for coverage here at the hospital as well as time to spend with each other. Right now, it is too fresh and we want to be by Mother's side."

"Alright, I understand and I love and appreciate you for your devotion. I don't know how your Mother and I were so blessed to have two girls like you. But, we will need our rest and we will need to have a plan that has some of you going home some of the time to sleep."

"Ok Dad," Laura and I both chimed in at the same time. As I look at Laura, tears are streaming down her face. Dad and I both reach out to give her a hug at the same time.

"We love you Dad," I said. "We will get through this together."

THE SATURDAY
BEFORE EASTER

CHAPTER 15

W hen we return to Mother's room, the whole gang is there. Pastor James has arrived and joined Collette, Adrienne, Amelia, Craig, Bob and Chris. Laura walks over to stand by Bob and they speak quietly, Bob updating Laura on his call with Robert and Alicia, and Laura no doubt sharing our conversation with Dad.

I hugged Pastor James and thanked him for coming. He also gave Dad a hug and asked quietly if he could lead the family in prayer since we are all present. Dad told him that we wouldn't have it any other way. Pastor James moved over and stood by the bed next to Mother.

"I have asked Dan if it is ok to lead the family in prayer and he has thanked me for being here with all of you and has assured me that a prayer together is desired. If I could get each of you to place one hand on the person next to you and one hand on Gloria," instructed Pastor James.

"Heavenly Father, we gather here today as your children; children of faith, believing in you as our Creator and Savior. As we stand today here before you, with our hands placed with each other and on Gloria, Father we ask that you be with us as we go through the next hours and days. Lord we ask for your wisdom, your guidance and your love to direct our thoughts, our words and our actions as we spend what may be the last days with this your faithful servant; Gloria. Father, you know that we love her and you better than any of us know the pain that each of us has endured watching her as she has declined in health over the last years. Lord we praise you for the spirit-filled family here that has stood by her side and sought your direction in every step of their lives. Lord we ask you to comfort us in this difficult time and ease the burden that comes with letting go of our beloved wife, mother, grandmother and friend. We ask this in your Holy name. Amen."

As each of us echoed the "Amen", there was not one dry eye in the room. Even Pastor James eyes were moist as he held both of Mother's hands and leaned over to place a kiss on one of her hands. Adrienne and Amelia were both just short of sobbing and I made my way over to them to hold them.

"Mom, we love her so much. It is going to be so hard to let her go," cried Adrienne.

"I know sweetie. Your grandmother is truly one of a kind. I am sorry that you don't remember her when she was in her prime. She was a true lady, a kind spirit and a wonderful Mom."

"Mom", Amelia added, "I know that she was awesome from all of the stories you have shared over the years. I think you are just like her in a lot of ways and I love you for that."

A new wave of tears started and I kissed both of my girls and told them I loved them beyond any possible measure and that I was so glad to have the two of them here tonight.

Dad started to speak just as Dr. Wilson walked in. Dr. Wilson began examining Mother and Amelia stepped closer to him to be available for any update that he may have on Mother's condition. After a brief examination, he indicated that he did not see any favorable change. He asked about Hospice and we confirmed that we had already met Anne Rogers and she was on-call as needed. Dr. Wilson reiterated that this could be hours or days and suggested that we as a family plan to get some rest.

"Dr. Wilson, we have most of our family here now and a few more who will be making decisions about when to come," I stated.

"At least some of us will be here at the hospital around the clock and we would appreciate you and the nurses updating us if you see a substantial change in either direction on our Mother's status."

He promised he would and left the room. Since I had been the person with the most recent sleep, I suggested that Laura and her family take Dad and go back to his house. Amelia and Adrienne both immediately lobbied to stay with me at the hospital for the night. Everyone was agreeable to the suggestion and so Dad, Laura, Bob, and Chris left to go to Dad's house. Adrienne and I situated the chairs in the room so that we could be close to Mom and close to each other. Amelia walked Craig down to his car and returned ready to share the vigil with her sister and I. Pastor James and Collette also made their exit, but not before an emotional good-bye and a promise from me to call them day or night with any changes.

We were all three quiet for a while, my girls and I, watching Mom and lost in our own thoughts.

Adrienne spoke first; breaking the solitude that each of us had kept since sitting down.

"Mom, tell us some of your favorite memories of Grandma, the happy memories when Grandma was in her element and loving life."

I knew where this was coming from. Adrienne was so young when Mom got sick that she has had a hard time remembering what her Grandmother looked like, and acted like, before her illness.

"Mom was a dresser," I began. "In the sixties, when I was a girl, Mom had the most amazing clothes. Back then, ladies really dressed up. You didn't see women in jeans and T-shirts or even shorts and tank tops. Women dressed and they dressed well. Your grandmother was in a league of her own. She had hats and shoes to match every outfit and gloves for church on Sunday. Her clothes were very tailored and always pressed to a crease. On Dad's arm, she was a knock-out."

The girls were smiling and watching their grandmother. I knew that telling the stories helped them to picture her as a vibrant, fun, and happy person; something that she had not been in a long time. I continued. "One of the really cool things about Mom was that she was so talented. She could hear a song one time and play it through on the piano or organ. She could read music and play anything, but it was the ability to hear a song and then play it without sheet music that was so amazing. I would labor over my piano lessons, struggling to get my brain and fingers moving at the same time, and she could just belt the songs out with what seemed to me to be absolutely no effort."

The girls were smiling and Amelia began laughing at her own piano lessons. The lessons had pretty much been a flop from the get-go. Amelia had always been the child with the running shoes, not the sit-still and practice on the piano kind of kid. Adrienne on the other hand had done really well with piano lessons. To this day, she is quite talented on the piano and even played the harp for a time in high school.

"Adrienne, do you still play the piano? Do you have anywhere that you can play?" I ask.

"Not so much really. One of my friends, Bethany Harper, has a piano in her apartment but I usually meet her for dinner or at the tennis courts. Occasionally I will play on the piano at church, when no one is around, but that doesn't happen very often."

As we sat, we continued to share stories about Mom, her life, her parents and what I knew about her growing up years. The girls marveled at how ambitious Mom had been and how much she had accomplished for a time when most women didn't go to college. It was a great moment. One that I knew I would remember for years.

Three generations of women, the younger ones embracing their grandmother for her success; as a Mom, as a wife, as a daughter and as a grandmother; all while being very involved in her work, her charity, her service to the church and her faith.

After the conversation lulled, I asked the girls if they wanted to sing quietly to their grandmother. When they were younger, and Mom was declining but still able to interact with those around her, the three of us would sing to her; and sometimes she would join in the song. Both of my girls are gifted singers, and our harmony with practice is pretty good.

Adrienne was the first to respond. "Mom, I think that would be great, but should we sing in a hospital at 1:00 in the morning? Isn't that a little rude?"

"I think it will be okay honey if we are very quiet. The door is closed so I don't think anyone will hear us."

"I want to sing Amazing Grace," said Amelia. "I think we do that one really well and grandma always joined in on that one when we sang it."

"Amazing Grace it is then. Who wants second soprano and who wants alto?" I asked.

"I will take Alto," offered Adrienne. The truth is all three of us could sing all three parts but in all of our singing for an audience in the past, the girls had always wanted me to sing the melody. They preferred the harmony.

As we each hum our first note to get in key, a chill makes its way down my back. As sad a time as this is, I also realize pure joy. Joy in spending this quality time with my girls, joy in knowing that they care about being here with their grandmother, wondrous joy as they each prepare to sing for their dying grandmother and joy in the praise that comes from this hymn.

As we start this favorite hymn, we each place our hands on my Mother. As I touch her forehead and then her cheek, I can tell that her fever is up. She is not alert, or possibly even awake, but the melody that she loves so much continues.

When we finish, both of the girls are smiling. I expect tears, but see smiles. A wave of fatigue, mixed with an air of sadness comes over me. We situate our chairs again so that we can each sit side by side with our feet on the bedrails and arms intertwined. I suggest that we try to take a nap and the girls agree. As we fall into a time of quiet, I pray a humble prayer of thanksgiving. As I finish the prayer, my tears threaten to spill over. I miss Roger so much right now that the loneliness for his touch is almost unbearable. As I finally doze off, I think about Roger watching as his three girls share such an important time together. I know he is smiling.

CHAPTER 16

I look at my watch for the hundredth time in the last hour. As I sit with Mom while Amelia and Adrienne nap, I can't seem to focus on any one subject. Flight of ideas, the technical description for what I am experiencing. I want to settle down and focus on all of the things we need to do, people we need to contact, etc.; but I just can't get my brain to land long enough on any one topic to accomplish much.

One of the things that I have been doing for the last few months is creating memory bookmarks in my brain of times when Mom was healthy and busy with life. I have been making a focused effort because it has been so long since she was in that phase of life, that it is easier to remember more recent times. Although we have had to make this journey of failed health with her, it is not the legacy of memories that I want to have of her. The effort is working. Over the past months my mental quest has taken me to times long since forgotten.

One of my favorite 'new memories,' is a time when Mother was probably in her mid-forties and I was maybe twelve or thirteen. I had wanted to go to a pool party in a location that was questionable from Mom and Dad's point of view. I guess I pouted (or ranted) about how everyone else was going to be there and I was being left out because my parents weren't hip enough to understand. They finally gave in and Mom took me to buy a new swim suit. The one I wanted was white eyelet lace with a bright pink bow woven through the eyelet at the bust line. The top opened at the bottom to show just a bit of skin. I knew the skin peeking out was too much for her and I knew it would be too much for my father, but I pleaded anyway. Mom thought for a minute and then told me she thought I looked pretty in it and that we would buy it. I was so ecstatic! I didn't feel like I had won a battle, I felt that Mom thought I was pretty and that made me feel special. What a great memory to add to the list of others that I had been digging up.

I look at my watch again; 3:45am. As I get up to stretch, Mom moves slightly and utters a small groan. I walk the two or three steps to the bed and put my hand on her forehead. She is burning up. I go in the bathroom and soak a wash cloth in cool water, wring it out and put it on her forehead. I open the drawer to get a mouth swab to move over her lips, which look dry and chapped.

Mom opens her eyes and tries to make a sound. Sometimes when she does this, I think she has forgotten that she can't communicate. It is weird, but I feel like she is surprised that nothing comes out.

"Mom, how was your nap?" I asked. "I put a cloth on your forehead to cool you down. I hope it helps you feel better."

Adrienne and Amelia both awaken and close in on each side of the bed in swift unison.

"Mom, what is going on?" asked Adrienne.

"Your grandmother just opened her eyes and I thought I would check on her. She still has a temperature so a cool cloth on her forehead should help her."

Amelia was stroking her grandmother and looking under the sheet at her skin. As she placed the cover back over Mother's feet, she looked at me and then at her grandmother. As she moved around to the head of the bed, she spoke with calmness and sensitivity, providing me with a brief glimpse of how she must interact with her patients.

"Grandma, how are you doing? Did you know that you, Mom, Adrienne and I all had a sleep-over in your room? We sang songs and told stories. It was like old times," Amelia stroked her grandmother's head as she spoke.

Adrienne reached up and rubbed her grandmother's shoulder at the same time. "Grandma, Mom told us about all of your fancy dresses, hats, gloves and shoes. I think I would have liked to be a woman in the sixties. You all did it right! Today, everybody is casual and I don't think it is as much fun."

I watch Mother as two of her granddaughters stroke her and talk to her. Her cheeks are flushed, the fever at work. Her eyes are vacant, the look we have all come to know. Her brow is furrowed, a perpetual sign of the confusion that must dominate her days. Yet, my girls have the love and patience to be present for her. To be sensitive and caring, touching and caressing while they chatter about the stories of their grandmother that they would remember and most likely retell to their own children one day.

I hear steps in the doorway and look over to see Dad standing there. He is taking it all in; his granddaughters in their health and vitality, and his wife as she ends her life on earth. I watch him a moment before he notices me in the corner. I can tell from his expression that he too will remember this sight; his granddaughters being there for their grandmother. As he wipes his hand over his mouth in a likely gesture of personal and emotional preparation, I see a quick moment of vulnerability and then with shoulders pulled back and hands outstretched, he walks to the bed and curls both girls in a hug. They are hugging him back with gusto. What a beautiful thing.

"What about me?" I asked. "Don't I get a hug?" Both girls reach over to include me in the embrace and Dad kisses me on the cheek.

Dad reaches over to Mom and kisses her good morning. She opens her eyes slightly and looks at him. As he holds her hand, he tells the three of us to go home and get some rest.

"I need some quiet time with your Grandma and I think you girls need some sleep. Laura was up when I left and I imagine she will be along in an hour or so. You girls run along. Mom and I will be just fine."

The girls and I spoke briefly and decided that Amelia would go to her apartment and Adrienne and I would head to my condo. It was 4:30 am and most likely Laura would be along any time to be here with Dad. As we kissed Mom and Dad good-bye and walked down to the cars, we agreed to meet again for lunch at Captain Harry's at 1:00 and then come back to the hospital.

As Adrienne and I slipped in to my car, both of us leaned our heads against the headrest and let out an audible sigh. As much as we loved being with Mother, we both knew that we were mentally and emotionally exhausted.

I back out of the parking space and put the car in drive. As we head home, we are both quiet, lost in our own thoughts. I can't help but wonder if I am driving away from the last time I will see my mother alive. The thought of that shakes me to the core.

If it were just me, I would have circled the parking lot and gone back inside. But it wasn't just me. I had Adrienne and she needed me and I needed her. The needs we have are not defined, but surely felt. Our experience with death and grief has given us a history from which to begin to understand this; the loss of someone we love.

Just before entering the traffic I text Laura to let her know that we are leaving and Dad is with Mom. Although he wants some time with her and would enjoy a brief time alone, he will need Laura to lean on as the day progresses.

Laura responds almost immediately indicating that she and Bob are going to be on their way in about fifteen minutes. Perfect.

CHAPTER 17

The music tone of my cell phone is ringing to the melody Adrienne programmed yesterday for Dad's calls. I grab the phone off of the nightstand and answer. Although it is Dad's ring, Laura is on the line. As I say 'hello', I look at the time; 9:45am.

"Becky, Mom has taken a turn for the worse and Dad wants me to let you know. Her breathing is shallow and the nurse believes that she is nearing her time. Dad said that if you are up to it, he would like to have you here."

"I am on my way."

I had showered when Adrienne and I got home, so I literally pulled on a denim skirt and a long sleeve polo shirt, slid my feet in to Nike mules and head for Adrienne's room. As I enter the hallway, she is coming out of the bathroom adjacent to her room.

"I heard the cell phone Mom, what is going on?"

"Mom has taken a turn for the worse and I need to get to the hospital right away. Do you want to stay here and have Amelia come get you later or do you want to go with me now?"

"Mom, I want to go with you. I will be ready in two minutes."

"Grab your suitcase too. We may need to hang out at Dad's for a while."

As Adrienne quickly changed, I sat on the couch and prayed; prayed for Mom, Dad and our family as we go through these next hours and days. Then I picked up my cell to call Amelia.

Amelia answered on the first ring. "Mom, what is it?"

I noted that she didn't even sound sleepy, a result of her training most likely, needing to go from sleep to awake on a moment's notice.

"Amelia honey, I am sorry to wake you but Laura just called and it seems as if Mom has taken a turn and they feel she may be in her final stages."

"Mom, I am on my way. Did they say anything else?"

I relayed the brief information that Laura had shared and promised to meet Amelia at the hospital. As she and I said our goodbyes, Adrienne came in the living room ready to go.

We quickly left the apartment and headed to the car. We are both quiet and I reach for Adrienne's hand. We walk hand in hand the rest of the way to the car. I am so glad that she is here, with me. I feel that it is important to her as well and quickly remember the nagging in my head on the way home from the airport last night. I make another quick mental note for me to spend some time with her, and see if I can find out what, if anything is bothering her.

My vehicle, a BMW SUV, is parked in the garage assigned to my condo. As we back out of the garage, Debbie Byrd is walking across the drive. She is waving and I stop next to her just long enough to bring her up to date on Mother's condition. Debbie assures us that if we need her to do anything she will be there day or night. I thank her as we pull away and out on to Gulf Drive.

Debbie had moved in about two years ago following a divorce from her husband of twenty-five years. She stayed busy with her job as an accountant, but she and I had spent some time poolside over the last two years.

So many of the owners in the condos are older and retired; it is nice to have someone closer to my age, someone who is working in the area, to share thoughts and experiences.

Adrienne is tense as we drive and I reach over to hold her hand. She looks over at me and I can see the worry, fatigue and sadness reflected in her eyes.

"Adrienne honey, are you okay?" I asked.

"I am okay Mom, just sad. I know it will be better for Grandma if she leaves this ugly disease, but I worry about you and Granddad. It will be hard for you to be here without her."

"It will. Taking care of your Grandmother has been your Grandfather's work for the last 20 years. All of the things that he was involved in before she got sick have moved on without him. But you know what? Your grandfather is strong. He has been by your Grandmother's side the whole way and he feels good about that. When he feels comfortable, he will have a chance to choose some new interests, hobbies or charities to fill his time."

"What about you, Mom? Isn't it going to be hard for you?"

"Adrienne, it will be different. I am ready for your grandmother to leave this world. She has suffered so much and it has been difficult to watch. I want relief for her and that in turn will bring relief to me." As I spoke the tears began to well up and spill over. I smiled through the tears at Adrienne and finished with, "Your grandfather and I will be okay."

The drive to the hospital on this Easter weekend was painful. Every nook and cranny along the shoulders of the road had a car parked on it. Beach-goers were everywhere and several times we were literally parked for a few minutes just to accommodate the crowds. As we turn to go over the bridge, I mentally count the number of green/red cycles on the stop light that will be required before we can actually make it across the bridge. Best case scenario based on the line of cars ahead of us, at least three cycles; maybe even five. My patience wearing thin, I try to breathe.

"Mom, what if we don't get there in time? Will you be upset?" Adrienne asked.

"We are going to get there Adrienne. But the answer to your question is no. I want to be there for Dad, but God has his own time and he is all-knowing. We will rely on His favor and grace to tend to those who are with Mother when she passes." Although that statement was true, the daughter in me wanted to be there for my father. I tap a little harder on the steering wheel.

Finally, we are over the bridge and almost to the turn in front of the hospital. As we wait at the traffic light, I see Amelia's car. Amelia doesn't see us so Adrienne texts her to tell her that we are right behind her and to wait for us in the parking lot.

As the three of us enter the building, we see Chris in the lobby. He says that his grandfather has sent him down to the gift shop for a pack of crackers; the kind with peanut butter in between the cracker layers. These are one of my Dad's favorites. Chris joins us and we head up to Mom's room. Chris tells us that his father picked him up at Dad's house about an hour ago, about the same time that we received Laura's call. He also said that Robert and his family are going to be leaving Charlotte this afternoon and they will be down here at least through Monday. He also relayed that Laura has spoken with Alicia and she is emotional and distraught about being away from the family. She and her husband Kevin are trying to figure out what their plans are and will call back this afternoon.

Chris is clearly a little shaken so I put my arm around him. I know he does not want to me to coddle him and so I thank him for letting us know and reassure him how glad we are that he is here with us to support the family.

When we walk in to Mother's room, the number of people in the room is surprising. Dad, Laura, Bob are there, along with Pastor James, Collette, and Maxine Banks. Standing in the corner is a gentleman that I recognize; John Stillman, head of the local hospice.

I hug everyone as I walk through the room and stop in front of John, hand out to greet his handshake.

"Hi John," I said. "It is nice to see you."

"Hello Becky, I hope you don't mind but I spoke with Anne Rogers earlier today and she gave me an update on your Mother's condition. I stopped by to see if there is any assistance that I can provide and to offer my sincere interest in helping your family in any way."

"John, that is very kind of you. We appreciate your concern and your time to stop by and introduce yourself to the family."

As I look around the room, I walk over to Mother's bed. I put my hand out to hold hers and reach down and whisper in her ear, "I love you Mother."

I can hear her shallow, raspy breath, and also notice her pale color. She is clearly in a deep sleep and seems to try very hard to take each breath.

Dad puts his arm around me and asks me if I am okay. I put my arm around him as well and fight back tears that I know will come if I give them permission.

"I am okay Dad."

Maxine and John Stillman both excuse themselves, sensing most likely that this is a time for family to share and be alone with Mom. I thank both of them for coming and then the girls and I lean on the window sill in the room, since the three chairs are taken. Chris is leaning against the wall. Dad sits down on the end of Mother's bed, next to her feet and places his hand on her leg.

Collette and Russell are standing at the head of the bed and Collette shares with us that food is being delivered to Dad's this afternoon. The ladies of the church have not only prepared a meal for today, but have also cooked several dishes that will be in the refrigerator for our convenience over the next week.

We all thank Collette and after the room is quiet. Amelia leaves the room, most likely checking on Mother's medical chart and also to speak with the nurses. Chris and Adrienne offer to go sit in the waiting area, as long as we promise to come get them if anything changes. Bob follows them, along with Collette and Russell. Dad, Laura and I are left together and Dad and I each sit in a chair next to Laura.

"I am so grateful to have you both here," Dad said. "Your Mother has declined in the last hour more than she ever has and I feel that we are very near the end."

"I agree Dad," I said. "I have never seen her condition this far along. I really believe that this is her time."

Laura's tears are running down her face and Dad puts his arm on her shoulder. I get up and sit next to Mom on her bed. I hold her hand and tell her I love her. I also give her permission to leave us. Many experts say that giving someone the permission to die is helpful to them in letting go of this life. I don't know if that is true or not, but in the event that it is, I want her to know that it is okay.

"Mom, you have been the most incredible Mother any girl could have. When you get to heaven, I am sure that a huge celebration will take place and God will tell you, "Well done, my good and faithful servant." We love you dearly, but if it is God's will for you to leave us soon we want you to go and not look back. We will see you in heaven."

I have tears streaming down my face but inside I feel an awesome release, a readiness, a transition to let her go and walk with God.

When I finished, Dad got up and sat on the other side of her bed, opposite me. Laura followed and sat on the bed by Mother's feet. I heard Amelia enter the room but stop short of coming further in the room. She would tell me later that she knew it was a moment that Dad needed with his wife and daughters.

"Gloria, you have been the love of my life for more than sixty years. I have loved you more than you will ever know and I have respected you as my wife, the mother of my daughters, but most of all for your faith and your walk with God. But Gloria, the doctors say that it is your time to leave us here and go be with God. I want you to do that Gloria. It is your reward for the life so well served here on earth," Dad gently said as he held her hand.

We were all in tears, including Dad, but for me it was emotion for the greatness of God and the celebration of heaven when we are finished here on earth.

That may be difficult for some to understand, and certainly is different from the emotion I felt at my husband's unexpected death, but with Mom we had been preparing for this day for a long time. Mom's diminishing personality, quality of life, and physical health had been painful to watch. Her end of life after so much suffering was a relief in so many ways.

I feel Amelia's hand on my shoulder and I turn around to include her in the moment. She has tears flowing down her face and as she squats next to me on the side of the bed she pats her grandmother's shoulder and kisses her good-bye. She asks where the others are and offers to go and join them.

As the minutes ticked by, we each sat lost in our thoughts. Anne Rogers came in and checked on Mother. She said that each situation is different but based on Mother's labored respirations; she believes that she will pass from this life soon. Anne assures us that she will be with us for the duration as she has fulfilled her other obligations here at the hospital.

"Anne, would you be willing to go down and speak with the rest of the family in the waiting room?" I ask. "My two girls are there and so is Laura's youngest son. They may ask questions of you that they wouldn't ask of us for fear of upsetting us. I just want to make sure that they have an outlet to discuss their questions or concerns as we go through these next hours."

Ann indicated that she would be happy to go and spend some time with them and would be back in the room as soon as she was finished there.

As we settle back in our positions by Mom, her breathing starts to change. At first it is barely noticeable, but in minutes her breathing is sharp and deep followed by silence. Laura leaves the room to go get the family and Dad leans over.

"It is okay Gloria. You are going to be okay. I will see you soon in heaven and we will celebrate the passing of this life together. I will miss you but time will pass quickly. I love you."

Just moments later she is gone.

As the family comes in to the room, each has a chance to say their last good-bye before the nurse comes in the room in response to the heart rate alarm. Since we have a DNR, do not resuscitate, code on Mother's chart, she simply slipped away. Time of death is 1:05pm.

The nurses ask us to leave the room, indicating that we can come back later to get her things. As we file from the room, I feel like I am leaving part of myself in that room, a part that I will never get back. Rationally I understand this, but my heart is longing.

Standing in the hallway, hugging and supporting each other, I look back at the closing door. It is a chapter ended; a life gone.

THE MONDAY
AFTER EASTER

CHAPTER 18

Mother's funeral was held on the Monday following Easter and was a beautiful testament to her life. Robert and his family arrived from Charlotte on Sunday morning and Alicia arrived alone on Sunday afternoon; her husband staying home with the children. This was the first time that Laura and I had been able to have our children together in over two years and although it was a time of grief, it was also a time for family, sharing memories and sharing the present together.

Robert's two children, Alex nine and Brooke seven years old, were a treat. Well mannered, but still kids, they softened the mourning in ways that only children can. On Monday as we were leaving the funeral, I was walking with Brooke and asked her how she was doing. She said she was doing fine and then after a moment she asked when we were going to the 'fun'eral. I told her I didn't understand and she told me that saying good-bye to her great grandmother wasn't fun and she thought it would be fun. When I asked her why she thought it would be fun, she explained that the word 'funeral' had the word 'fun' in it. Much of the car ride back to Dad's house was explaining that sometimes bigger words have smaller words in them but the smaller words may not mean the same thing inside another word. As an example, I used the word garage. Although it has the word 'age' in it, it doesn't have anything to do with one's age.

Adrienne was in the front seat with me and Brooke was in the backseat. Adrienne had a big grin across her face, clearly enjoying both Brooke and the distraction.

As the day went on, many friends stopped by Dad's house to give their condolences. Ladies from the church organized the constant influx of food and flowers, giving us the free time to spend with those visiting. Collette and Russell spent most of the day with us and it was so helpful to me to have them there.

Amelia and Craig hung close all afternoon, often sitting with or near Dad. I had asked Amelia to keep an eye on Dad today and to make sure that the service and all of the people were not too much for him. Dad would never be one to hold up the white flag of surrender and ask people to leave, or retreat to his room for some quiet time. She and I caught up mid-afternoon and she indicated that he was doing fine.

After the last guest left, Robert's wife Caitlin left with Chris in Laura's car to take the kids back to the hotel. Although there was room at Dad's house, Robert and Caitlin wanted to be able to keep the kids on a schedule and have a place to retreat if it seemed to be getting too much for them. Robert stayed behind to visit with the family and Chris would return as soon as he had them safely in their hotel room.

We all gathered in the family room and Dad was the first to speak.

"I want to thank you all for being here. Gloria would be so proud of all of you. I know she would want me to say that she loved each of you. Her funeral was beautiful and each of you being there made it more special. We have celebrated her today, but we have much more to celebrate in the months and years ahead. I want each of you to look forward, keeping your treasured memories, but placing your faith and families and all that is to come for us on the road ahead. We have a wedding in a few short weeks and I want this time to be about Amelia and Craig. Gloria would want that too." As he stood up, he continued, "I have had a long day and I am going to bed. Feel free to stay here as long as you like, you won't bother me."

As I stood to hug him goodnight, a line formed around me. Each of us hugged Dad as he headed off to bed.

After Dad had gone, we began to discuss plans for tomorrow. Amelia was off until Wednesday. Adrienne had called work and was taking the remainder of the week off on family bereavement time. Bob and Laura said they would most likely leave on Wednesday as well. Bob and Chris both had taken Monday through Wednesday off at work and both planned to be back in their respective offices on Thursday. Robert said that he and his family would probably leave tomorrow afternoon, indicating that it was easier to travel with the children when part of the trip was done during the night while they sleep. I hadn't confirmed my plans with Mary, but I would most likely take the rest of the week off with Adrienne; maybe going in to the office for an hour or two to sign documents and handle a few issues.

We decided that Adrienne and I would head back to my house and take Robert to his hotel on the way. Amelia and Craig would leave as well, since Craig has to be back to work tomorrow. We will all meet again here in the morning after breakfast to spend some time with Dad and Robert and his family before they leave.

After dropping Robert I receive a text from Amelia. I hand the phone to Adrienne so that she can read it and reply while I am driving.

"Mom," Adrienne said, "Amelia is coming over to your place. She wants to be with us."

"Text her back and tell her to meet us there. I will open a bottle of wine and we will relax a bit before bed," I suggested.

"She is *very* cool with that," Adrienne replied.

As we neared the turn for my building, I could see Amelia turning in behind us. It is clear that she literally dropped Craig, to manage to have caught up with us so quickly. As we get out of the cars and walk to the condo, I think for the first time, this is our new normal. For the moment, no one is sick, there is no emergency and the constant stress looming over my head as a family caregiver is absent. I am too tired to register the full effect yet, but I know that it feels different. I unlock the condo door and enter with my girls.

Amelia and Adrienne both sit down in the living room while I put my purse away and drop my shoes in the closet. Both girls opt for red wine so I select a bottle of merlot from the wine cabinet. I pour three generous glasses and Adrienne gets up from her chair to help carry the glasses to the living room. If nothing else, hopefully the wine combined with exhaustion will help us all sleep.

"Mom, how are you doing?" asked Adrienne.

"Honey, I am fine. I feel a little numb and pretty tired, but I am at peace. How are two doing?"

Amelia spoke up first. "I am sad and relieved I guess. Sad for us that Grandma is gone, but relieved because she suffered so much and you and Granddad had to watch her decline all these years. From that stand-point, I am relieved that it is over."

I look at Adrienne to see if she is going to respond. She looks at me. "Mom, I am just sad. I know Grandma suffered and I am glad it is over for her, but today when we were going through the funeral and you and Aunt Laura spoke about the kind of mother she was, all I could think about is I don't know how you can say goodbye to her like that. I mean the two of you were so composed. I don't know what I would do if someone told me I had to speak at your funeral when your time comes. It is sad and remarkable at the same time."

"Adrienne, it is a process. You can't relate right now because I am a healthy, working Mom. Going through the long duration of watching Mom decline is different than saying good-bye to a healthy Mom. But, I do know what you mean. If you would have told me twenty years ago that I could get up and give a eulogy for my mother's funeral, I would have told you "no way". God has worked on me in this illness. He has provided wings when I was falling and courage when I was failing. His love and grace has been amazing."

"Still Mom, you and Aunt Laura are amazing. I admire both of you so much," Amelia added.

I smile at them and reply, "Thank you for saying that. It means a lot to me for my daughters to be proud of their mother. You girls are everything to me and I appreciate you so much. I honored my mother today. It was my sincere honor to do it."

As we sipped wine, and reminisced about the day, I suddenly felt very tired. I listened as the girls chatted and the conversation moved on to discussion of Amelia's wedding.

"Mom," Amelia started, "Uncle Bob said that he really liked Craig. He said he thought he was a "stand-up" guy."

"That is great Amelia. Did anyone else have a chance to meet him and give you their thoughts?" I asked.

"Yes, Chris told me that he thought he was cool. They traded stories about psych cases. The ones Chris treats at the counseling center and the ones Craig flies around on a daily basis," Amelia said with a laugh.

Adrienne and I joined in the laughter as well. As we began talking about our plans for the remainder of the week, I could tell that we were all crashing; exhaustion finally taking over. We agreed that we would all go to Dad's in the morning to visit with the rest of the family and then in the afternoon, conquer some of our bridal 'to-do's'.

It was after 11:00 when we decided to go to bed, each girl to one of the spare bedrooms. I had the same feeling that I had on Saturday after Mother had passed away. A door was closed and the future lay ahead. In a weird way, I felt like I could take a deep breath and exhale hard. I was starting to understand the huge weight that was no longer perched on my shoulders. It wasn't yet relief, just awareness, a feeling of new beginning.

THE TUESDAY
AFTER EASTER

CHAPTER 19

When Adrienne, Amelia and I arrived at Dad's, it was clear that the family was more rested than any day in the last week. Chris and Bob had been for a run on the beach and looked refreshed and energized. Laura had cooked enough breakfast for an army; pancakes, eggs, bacon, biscuits, and blueberry compote for the pancakes.

"Laura, where did you get the blueberries to make this compote?" I asked. Laura and I were both great cooks, but I can assure you that I did not wake up this morning with making blueberry compote on the brain.

"They were in the center of a big fruit tray left last night and I thought they would be a nice addition to the pancakes."

"Well, pancakes are not usually on my diet, but guess what? The blueberry compote has pushed me over the edge," I admitted. As I took the first bite, an audible 'yum' followed.

"Laura, these are incredible. What is in this pancake batter?" I asked.

"Cinnamon. It is the cure of all things if you read the nutritional gurus these days. I just use it because it makes things taste better," she quipped.

In a matter of a few minutes the platter of pancakes was gone. My girls had been lured by the chatter and had each downed three of the tasty cakes themselves.

Robert, Caitlin and the kids walked in the door and both Amelia and I chimed at the same time, "Better make some more!"

Dad came in from outside to greet Robert and his family. He was so glad to see those small children. The realization hit me that my girls' children would never know their great grandmother and out of nowhere the tears welled up. I managed to head down the hall and away from the kitchen before anyone noticed the moment of emotion. I closed the bathroom door and chided myself to pull it together. I waited a few minutes, flushed the toilet, and put a smile on my face as I walked back in to the kitchen. There, Laura was piling high the next platter of pancakes for the kids. As the family enjoyed this time together, I sat back and relished the moment. Although there was a virtual hole in my day, a calendar spot that felt like a missed appointment with Mom now gone, this time together was good.

"Becky," Dad called from the pool deck. I walked outside to see what he needed.

"What is it Dad?" I asked.

"I want to take all those flowers that we have in the house up to the nursing home and gather Gloria's personal items. I am hoping maybe you and the girls will go with me."

"Dad, I would be happy to go and I am sure the girls will be too. Did you want to go now?" I asked.

"No, let's wait until Robert and his family are on the road. Do you have plans this afternoon?" Dad asked.

"Well, the girls and I are going to do some of our bridal things this afternoon before Amelia goes back to work tomorrow. But we can stop on the way, that is not a problem," I said.

"No, I want you girls to have that time. You go ahead and I will get Laura to go with me, unless you are planning to take her too." Dad said.

"I had planned to ask Laura to go but honestly I don't know if she will. Let me ask her and I will let you know. If she wants to go with us, we will all stop at the nursing home on the way. I am sure that there are many residents there that do not have any flowers. Maybe the volunteers could break up the arrangements and put some of them in the rooms that rarely have visitors."

"That is what I am thinking," Dad replied.

After talking with Laura, who absolutely wanted to go to the bridal shop, we all agreed that we would go with Dad to the nursing home prior to shopping. Around 11:00, Robert decided that they should begin their trip home. Brooke seemed to be coming down with a cold and they felt it best to go ahead and make an earlier start.

As we all said goodbye, we knew that we would see each other at the wedding in a few weeks. It had been so nice to get to see the kids and spend time with Robert and Caitlin. I wanted to get to know them better and be a bigger part of their lives. Now with less care-taking responsibilities, maybe a road trip to Charlotte and a flight to Denver are no longer out of the question. Although Robert and his family are tentatively planning to come back down for Amelia's wedding, Alicia and her family would not be able to make the wedding unless something changes.

As Robert and his family drove away, all of the girls got in my car and followed Dad, Laura and I to the nursing home in Dad's truck. Laura and I wanted to ride with Dad to make sure that he was okay and to be there if he needed to talk to someone.

Actually, not so surprising because it was Dad's way, he was in pretty good spirits. Using the flowers to cheer someone else was his style and with that came joy.

After seeing to Mother's things, dropping off the flowers, and accepting the love and condolences of the staff, we headed out to my car. Dad waved us off and assured us that he, Bob and Chris would get in to some mischief on their own. We doubted that there would be much mischief, but figured the sports channel might get some attention while we were gone.

As we crowded in to my SUV, spirits were light and anticipation of a wedding managed to divert our hearts and attention to a happier place.

CHAPTER 20

Amelia looked exquisite. She literally took my breath away in the beautiful dress that she had chosen to wear down the aisle to marry Craig. The dress style had a one shoulder drape from the right shoulder, with the left shoulder bare. The bodice of the dress was form-fitting with horizontal seaming under the bust. Stitched sequins and beads trimmed the bodice and followed the curve of the dropped waist. A full, flowing skirt completed the dress with satin and chiffon gleaming in the lights from the bridal salon's modeling area.

I looked at Laura and saw her smile of approval.

"Amelia, you could not have picked a more beautiful dress darling. You look like a dream. Craig is going to be over the moon when he sees you," Laura raved.

"Aunt Laura, thank you. What a nice thing to say. I hope he is over the moon—this dress is awesome!" Amelia replied.

Alicia and Adrienne were looking on appreciatively.

"Well, what do you ladies think?" Amelia asked Adrienne and Alicia.

"Amelia, it is so beautiful" Adrienne replied.

"A knock-out," Alicia chimed in.

"Great! That makes me feel better. You all are the only ones that are going to see the dress. So mum is the word. I really want to surprise Craig."

We all agreed to keep the fabulous dress a secret. As Amelia went to change, the sales clerk led Adrienne to her dressing room. It is really important to get the final fitting on Adrienne's dress since she will be out of town and this her last chance to try it on before the wedding.

Amelia came out after having changed from the dress just in time to see Adrienne exit the dressing room. Dressed in the most beautiful periwinkle blue dress, Adrienne is stunning. Her dark hair and fair skin a gorgeous contrast to the rich jewel tone.

"Adrienne, you look fabulous," Amelia said. "That dress is so becoming on you."

"Thanks Amelia. I really love it. Mom, what do you think?"

"Adrienne, you are just stunning. I love that color on you and the dress fits like a dream."

The dress is a taffeta blend, strapless style dress with an asymmetrical waistline that has been designed to flatter any figure. Adrienne totally rocks it. As I look at her in this dress and Amelia in her wedding dress earlier, I can't believe that these girls are so grown-up and beautiful.

"Adrienne, you are a vision in that dress," Laura stated. "That color should permanently be in your wardrobe. Buy anything you see in that shade. It reminds me of the finest tanzanite gemstone."

"Thanks Aunt Laura. I really love it too."

As the seamstress finalizes a few alteration details, Amelia and I look through the accessories to see if there is anything additional that we need. She has already purchased her shoes and she will be wearing her hair down with her veil which we have also purchased. The bridesmaid's gifts arrived during Mother's hospitalization, so that was another thing off of the list. I have not seen them but Amelia said that they will be perfect with the pale pink roses that the bridesmaids will be carrying.

As we finish the dress fittings at Wedding Royale, Adrienne requests that we make another stop.

"Mom, I really need a couple of scoops of ice cream from Henry's."

"You *need* a couple of scoops?" I asked playfully.

"Mom, I am in," assured Amelia. As she said that she turned to Aunt Laura and Alicia. "You guys remember Henry's don't you? They have fresh homemade ice cream every day that is to die for."

"Let's go," Alicia said. "I could use some fat and sugar, adult style. If I am in an ice cream shop, I have kids hanging all over me. This will be a double treat; great ice cream and adult company." With that, we all laughed and strolled the two blocks to Henry's ice cream shop.

As I walked with my daughters, my sister and my niece, I reflected on the grief process. Just yesterday we were saying good bye to Mother. Although our pain is real and our grief fresh, the process has been on-going for so long. The ice cream shop is a blessed diversion and a chance for us to connect, feel a moment of pleasure, and support each other in our presence and with our love.

Walking up the steps to our favorite ice cream shop, I put my arm around Amelia. "Sweetheart, you are going to be a beautiful bride. I can't wait to see you walk down the aisle in that amazing dress."

"Thanks Mom. I am so happy. It seems a little wrong to be happy when we just had Grandma's funeral, but I know she would be okay with this, looking forward to a happy time."

"I know she would honey. She would want these to be the best days of your life and she would want Adrienne and me to love every minute with you. And we will."

I smile through my watery eyes and give her a hug and kiss. "Now let's get some ice cream. I hope Henry has made some sinful chocolate recipe. If I am blowing the calories, I am going all out."

Adrienne is already at the front of the line. Henry has six freshly made flavors; Chocolate Mint, Hot Fudge Brownie, Caramel Pecan, Strawberry, Vanilla Bean and Raspberry Sorbet. Adrienne is getting two scoops; Hot Fudge Brownie and Caramel Pecan. She tells me that the combination is in honor of her favorite candy bar. Amelia is ordering the Raspberry Sorbet, one scoop, rationalizing that a scoop of actual ice cream might jeopardize the fit on her dress. Laura and Alicia both order Chocolate Mint and I order last with a scoop of Hot Fudge Brownie in a waffle cone. As we sit around and enjoy our cool treat, we coax Alicia in to telling us about her life in Denver, the kids, and Kevin's work.

As we leave the ice cream shop my cell phone rings. I do not recognize the number and answer on the third ring.

"Hello. A pause and then, "Yes John, it is nice to hear from you."

Another pause on my end and that is enough to stir curiosity for the group and stop their conversation so that they can listen to mine.

"No, I am sorry, I didn't see you at the funeral yesterday but it was very nice of you to come." Another pause followed by, "Thank you very much. That means a lot to me." Another moment and then, "Thank you so much. Good-bye."

"Who was that?" Amelia asked.

"It was John Stillman, the Director of Hospice. Apparently he was at the funeral yesterday, although I didn't see him. He said he sat in the back of the church."

"What else did he say Mom?" Adrienne asked. "It sounded like the call was more personal."

"Well, he paid all of us a nice compliment. He said that it has been a long time since he has seen a family so engaged and involved in both the day to day care and the visitation at the hospital. He said that he wanted to make sure that he told us that, but felt that yesterday was not the right time."

"That was so nice of him to call," Laura said. "I am sure he sees all types of families and situations. It must be a tough job, knowing that each day you get up you are dealing with death and the grief of a family."

"I don't know," I replied. "I think it would be meaningful work. Helping families cope with the end of life could be really rewarding. I mean, at the end of the day, he and his staff have touched people in very special ways. I admire them for making this their life's work."

"I couldn't do it," replied Laura, "so I sure am glad there are the John's and Anne's of the world. I am grateful for them."

I realize that this talk is channeling the group down the sad road again and quickly reversing the light moments of ice cream and girl time. I come up with a suggestion to try to recapture the mood.

"Before we go back to Dad's, I suggest we go stick our toes in the sand. Is anyone game for a walk on the beach down by the pier?"

A unanimous yes resounded and we once again crammed in to my SUV for the short drive to the beach. As we leisurely drove in the direction of the beach, Amelia began telling Laura and Alicia about the wedding party and her history with each of the bridesmaids. Adrienne added commentary, inserting details on each of the girls. Four bridesmaids and Adrienne as Maid of Honor; it is a big wedding. And it is just around the corner. In fact, the big event is just seven weeks from this Saturday. Time is flying.

As I drive I can't believe how excited I am about the wedding. It is Amelia's time and I will do everything I can to make sure that it is special. Once again, I miss Roger so much. He would have wanted to see his oldest daughter walk down the aisle by his side. Instead, he will watch it from heaven and Dad will walk her down the aisle. As I park the car alongside the sidewalk to the pier, I blink back the tears that threaten.

One day at a time Sweet Jesus. Hopefully I will get these emotions back in check before the big day. A crying mother will not make for good wedding pictures.

"We are here," I said. "It looks like the Easter crowd has cleared out a little. That is good."

Although tourism is Florida's primary industry, the crowds at the beaches during spring break can get a little out of hand. Scanning the beach, there are a few fishermen on the pier, two or three couples walking and a family with small children further down the beach. Otherwise, we have the place to ourselves.

CHAPTER 21

D ad, Bob and Chris had in fact kept the sports channel on while we were gone and Dad and Bob were both napping when we arrived. Chris was on his laptop reading email and catching up on his social networking. It was almost 6:00 and I suggested that the girls and I get some dinner heated up from the array of options brought yesterday by members of the church and family friends. Chris indicated that Collette and Reverend James had stopped by earlier in the afternoon. They dropped off a chicken casserole that was in the kitchen and still warm, along with a Caesar salad. That would be perfect for dinner so the girls and I, along with Laura and Alicia, began getting the food ready for dinner.

Just as we were putting food on the table, there was a knock on the front door and Maxine came in carrying a cake pan and cover.

"Hello everyone," Maxine greeted. "I had some time on my hands today and wanted to try out a new recipe. I hope you don't mind testing it out for me," smiling as she spoke. "It is a chocolate cheesecake with a toasted coconut and graham cracker crust. I thought it sounded good and I am hoping you enjoy it."

"We will Aunt Maxine," Amelia said. "But only on one condition and that is that you stay and have some with us. We are just getting ready to eat. Would you like a plate?"

"Oh no Amelia, honey. I ate earlier and I don't allow myself to eat this late in the day. But, I will stay and visit and maybe taste that cake."

As Maxine was talking she went over and gave Adrienne a hug.

"Adrienne, I miss you so much. It is so good to see you. I can't tell you how often you are on my mind."

"Thank you Aunt Maxine. I miss you too."

As we sat down to dinner, Dad insisted that Maxine sit with us while we eat, rather than on the kitchen stool where she had planned to sit. The casserole was excellent and Aunt Maxine's cake was delicious. None of us mentioned to her the afternoon stop at the ice cream shop. I couldn't remember the last time I enjoyed two decadent desserts in the same day.

"Alicia, what time is your flight tomorrow," Laura asked.

"It is at 10:30 tomorrow morning. Do you think you; Dad and Chris can drop me on your way out of town?"

"Of course we can. What time do you think that you need to be there in order to get your bag checked and get through security?" Laura asked.

"I think if I am at the airport by 9:00 that should be good. But if you want to leave earlier in the morning, that is ok with me too. I can hang out in the airport, have coffee and read a book or something."

"No, we won't need to do that. If we leave here about 8:15, that should work for everyone. That will get you to the airport in time and have us back in Atlanta before dark."

"Okay Mom, that sounds good to me."

During the conversation Dad disappeared to his bedroom and he returned holding a box. He asked us to clear the dinner table and then come back and sit down. The girls and I cleared the table and loaded the dishwasher. Laura and Alicia went back to their respective bedrooms to get a head start on packing. Within twenty minutes, we were all back at the table.

"All of the girls in the family are here tonight and I thought it would be a good time to give you each something of your mother's or grandmother's as the case may be. Gloria didn't have a chance to give her opinion on who should have what, but I have given it a lot of thought in the last few days. I have tried to think about each of you and the characteristics that you have of her and pick something based on what I think she would want me to give and what she would want you to have of hers."

"Laura, you were our first born and I remember the day that we came home from the hospital with you. You were so tiny and neither of us really knew what we were doing." Dad smiled at Laura and then at Alicia. "I want you to have the first real piece of jewelry that I ever gave your mother, other than her wedding band. As her first-born, the first jewelry present should be yours." With that Dad handed Laura the strand of pearls that he gave mother as a wedding present. Laura had tears in her eyes as she got up from the table and gave Dad a hug.

"Dad, I will cherish these. I know that Mother loved to wear them and I promise to take good care of them and pass them on some day to Alicia. Thank you Dad."

"Becky, you entered this world early in the morning and we have had to get up early in the morning every day since to keep up with you. You have been there for us through all of this day by day. I thank you for that. I think Gloria would want you to have her ruby ring. I gave her this ring when you were born. We knew that we would not be able to have any other children and I bought it for her to honor her as the mother of my children."

With that, Dad handed me the ruby ring that Mother had worn in the early days of their marriage. She had received many other pieces of jewelry over the years, but the ruby ring held special sentiment for her and I am so honored to have it.

"Thank you Dad. This means so much to me and I think Mom would love that you are doing this and that you put so much thought and consideration in to the choices. I love you so much."

"Amelia, you were our first granddaughter. What an amazing day. We were so worried about your mother making it through the delivery okay and then when we saw you, all worries were gone. You were such a beautiful baby."

"Thank you Granddad," Amelia said as she got up from her chair and came around the table to hug Dad.

"Since you are getting married here in a few weeks, I thought that Gloria would have wanted to give you something to wear on your wedding day. I thought about the "something old, something new, something borrowed and something blue" and I decided to give you Gloria's blue sapphire ring. She loved this ring and it is contemporary enough for a young beautiful woman like you to wear."

"Granddad, I would be so honored to wear this ring on my wedding day. I wanted to wear something of Grandma's anyway, so that I would feel like she was there with me. Thank you."

"You are welcome."

"Alicia, you were our second granddaughter and Gloria and I didn't make it in time for your birth. You came a week early and your Grandmother and I couldn't get there quick enough. When we did see you though, you were beautiful. Gloria said that you were "magnificent". I remember that was the word that she used; magnificent. I thought about what Gloria would want for you and I decided that she would love for you to have her charm bracelet. She collected those charms to commemorate important milestones in her life. It tells a story, a part of her story. Alicia you have moved the greatest distance from our family. You are creating your own story with your husband and beautiful children. I want this to remind you of your grandmother's milestones as a woman. She would love you, Kevin and your children. I am sorry that they will not get a chance to know her."

Alicia had tears streaming down her face as she took the bracelet from her Grandfather.

"Granddad, this is the most special gift and I will always cherish the story you told me tonight and Grandmother's bracelet. Someday when Elise is old enough, I will tell her this story just the way you told me. I have a picture of Grandma when she won the music award. I will keep both of these things together so that I can keep them safe for Elise to have and treasure when she grows up."

"Adrienne, you were our last granddaughter and I will never forget the day you were born. You were so beautiful and looked like a little dark hair cherub. We couldn't have loved you more."

Adrienne had also walked over to her grandfather and had her arm around him as he continued to talk.

"I think Gloria would want you to have her cross necklace. As you know, she wore this cross almost every day. I think she would want you to know that God is always with you; no matter where you are and that you are never alone, even though you have moved away from us and are out on your own.

"Granddad, I will put this on and wear it close to my heart. Thank you. That was such a beautiful sentiment. I wish we had videoed this."

Everyone nodded in agreement. A video of this would have been an incredible keepsake.

Dad seemed touched by the girls' responses and content with his decisions. It had to be hard on him to say goodbye to Mom and part with things that represented so much of their history together, yet at the same time, sharing these things will allow them to be part of our future. It was a loving moment which Dad quickly moved away from by backing up his chair and heading to the living room.

"Chris, your day will come. I have already set aside some things for you and Robert. Tonight was the girls' night. I wanted them to have something of their grandmother's that they could keep for a lifetime."

"I think that was a really great thing to do Granddad. That was very touching and such a personal moment."

"Thanks Chris. Your grandmother loved you so much. She would have been proud of the man that you have become."

"Thank you Granddad."

After another hour of visiting, Amelia, Adrienne and I left to give Laura and her family some alone time with Dad and then get some rest in anticipation of their long drive back to Atlanta and Alicia's flight back to Denver. Amelia's car was still at my condo, so we all rode together back to my house. Amelia received a call earlier from Craig and he planned to be back in town late tonight. Since she will be working a ten hour shift tomorrow, she needs to get back to her condo so that she can get some sleep.

As we drove we talked about how thoughtfully Dad had delivered these messages of love and what a tribute it was to Mom that he had clearly been so deliberate in making each gift personal. Dad's generous spirit was truly an extraordinary moment for us.

As we reach the condo, Amelia decides to go directly home rather than come inside for a while. Although the day has been a good one, we are still emotionally exhausted from all that has gone on in the last week and the lure of a good night's sleep was calling us.

Once inside, Adrienne and I agree that a bed and about eight hours of sleep is long overdue. We briefly discuss plans for tomorrow and agree that we will sleep late if possible and then go for a nice walk on the beach before going back over to Dad's to check on him. After that, the day is open and I am hoping to get some good one on one time with her. The tugging at the back of my mind that something is not right has not dissipated over the last few days. Although she seems better, less distracted, I just have that mother's intuition that she has something on her mind.

As I lie down in my bed and pick up my Bible for some devotional time, I thank God for the day we have had today. I love spending time with my sister, her daughter and my daughters. Dad's personal time tonight with each of us was so special and such a blessing. What a wonderful day; a day that I will remember for many years to come.

PART 2

EARTHLY TRANSITIONS

Jeremiah 29:11

"For I know the plans I have for you," declares the Lord, "plans to prosper you and not to harm you, plans to give you hope and a future."

THE WEDNESDAY
AFTER EASTER

Chapter 22

I awoke Wednesday morning to the smell of coffee. I slipped on my flip-flops and walked in to the kitchen to see Adrienne fully showered and dressed.

"Good morning Mom. Did you sleep well?"

"Yes, I did. I cannot believe it is almost 9:00. I don't remember the last time I slept past 6:00 or 7:00 in the morning."

"Well, I am sure you needed your sleep. You have been going non-stop since Grandma got sick."

"That is true, but still. How long have you been up? I didn't even hear you shower or get dressed."

"I woke up around 7:00 and went out on the balcony for a while. It was so beautiful to sit and watch the waves and the sea birds. I really miss this place."

As Adrienne poured our coffee, she seemed relaxed and rested. One small knit between her eyebrows might represent some worry or fatigue, but otherwise she looked good.

"Let's take our coffee on the balcony," I suggested. "I could use some of that relaxation you picked up this morning."

We sat in the chairs that overlook a stretch of the Gulf of Mexico, as far as you can see. As we sip our coffee, we both take in the scenery. An older woman with a white beach hat is walking her poodle along the shoreline. A young, athletic man is running in the opposite direction, shirtless with a perspiration sheen covering his exposed upper body. Further down the beach we see two golden lab retrievers chasing Frisbees tossed by a young couple dressed in workout clothes. A few sun-worshipers are already in reclining chairs, prepared to soak in the morning rays. It is a peaceful place to sit and Adrienne and I are quiet as we absorb the surroundings and reflect privately on our own thoughts.

Finally, I break the silence.

"Adrienne, you and I have hardly had any time together to just sit and visit. Tell me how things are going for you."

"Mom, things are going great. Work is good. I have my friends and I stay busy. The apartment isn't the greatest, but I only have a few more months on the lease and then I can figure out what I want to do from there."

"Are you thinking of moving once the lease is up?"

"Yes. I don't know where yet, but I am starting to think about it and weigh the options."

"Is there a location that you would prefer over where you are now? You are pretty close to your work and church."

"I like the location, but the apartment complex just isn't working for me."

"Why is that?"

"Well, mostly it is just that the tenants are young and the amount of partying and rowdy noise is too much. The majority are still in college and are still in that 'stay drunk and loud phase' that I don't relate to at this point in my life. I would rather be with the young career types. People who have moved on from that stage of their life and are now getting serious about work and family."

"I understand. That makes sense. Have you checked any other locations that might be of interest?"

"Not yet. I have time. My lease isn't up until August."

"So what else is going on? Have you been dating anyone since you quit seeing Sean?"

Adrienne and Sean had been dating for a few months when Sean decided to take a job in Portland. Although he asked Adrienne to consider moving with him, she quickly put an end to that discussion, understanding that the relationship was way too new to make that type of commitment.

"No. Not really. I mean, there is one guy that I really like a lot but we have only been out a couple of times. I am not sure if the relationship is going anywhere yet, but we are supposed to go out again when I get back home."

"Really? Tell me about him."

"His name is Andre Engel. His father is from Germany and his mother is American. He was born in a small town in Germany and lived there until he was ten years old. His parents moved to the U.S. to be near his mother's parents who were both sick. Anyway, I met him through one of my co-workers at a party. He is a really nice guy and really cute." Adrienne smiled as she added the last sentence.

"He sounds wonderful. What does he do for a living?"

"Right now he is in transition. His degree is in international law and he worked for a patent firm in Washington D.C. He moved to Charlotte to start another job but the job fell through. He has some applications out but he is really hoping for one specific job. He should know in the next few weeks whether he gets it or not."

"Tell me what you like about him."

"He is funny, obviously very smart, but mostly he is kind. He is a strong Christian and very devoted to volunteering his time for charities. You would really like him Mom, but I don't want to get ahead of myself. We have been on a few dates, but haven't made any kind of dating commitment to each other, so it is too soon to get excited about him. I was thinking about asking him to be my date at the wedding. What do you think?"

"I think that if you would enjoy his company, and it sounds like you would, then you should definitely invite him."

"I am thinking about it. I just don't want people to think that it is more than it is. Right now we are just starting to date and I don't want people marrying us off when they see us together at a wedding."

I couldn't help but laugh. Although Adrienne had a point, and no doubt there would be a few people who would be doing just that, her expression of fear and foreboding was funny.

"Don't laugh Mom! You know I hate to be center of attention. That is Amelia's forte, not mine. And it is her day anyway. I would like to have him at the wedding but I am just not sure that it is worth it."

"Well, you have time to make up your mind. Since you will be driving, airfare for him is not an issue and actually I would like for you to have someone riding with you."

"I talked with Robert about following him and his family down, but you know how that goes. Trying to stay together for that distance is too hard. Besides, I will want to come earlier and stay longer than he will so the timing doesn't work."

"Well, if you decide to bring Andre, I look forward to meeting him. Your decision sweetheart, do what your heart tells you to do."

"So, what else is going on? Call me crazy, but I would swear that you have had something on your mind while you have been here. Mother's intuition or gut working overtime. Care to share?"

"Honestly Mom, I have a few things going on but I don't think this is the time."

"Of course it is the time. If you need to talk through something or if you are worried about something, I want to be there for you. You know that."

"I know Mom, but you have been through a lot over the last week or so and this isn't that important. We can talk about it later."

"Nope, we are talking now. What is up?"

"Ugh, I don't know if I want to get in to this right now."

"Get in to what? Adrienne, you are worrying me. What is it?"

"Mom, let me get you another cup of coffee. I think you are going to need it."

As Adrienne stood up with both coffee cups and headed to the kitchen, I thought my heart was going to jump out of my chest. *What could be going on with her?*

I watch her from the balcony as she fills the cups and grabs two fruit flavored yogurts from the refrigerator and two spoons from the cabinet drawer. *How in the world does she think I am going to eat when my throat is closed off from sheer worry?*

Adrienne placed the cups and yogurt cartons in front of us and opened one. As she dug her spoon in the blueberry mixture, she looked at me and then back down at her breakfast.

"Mom, I was going to talk to you about this when I came home this weekend, but that was before Grandma got sick and then passed away. Given those events, it just didn't seem appropriate."

"Go ahead Adrienne tell me what is going on."

"Well, about four weeks ago, I was approached by an organization called Children's NuDawn. They are a non-denominational not for profit based out of Miami. They have been around about eight years and primarily work in Europe and South Africa. They do have operations in Miami and New York, but those are mostly administrative."

My cell phone interrupts Adrienne with Dad's new programmed ring tone. I tell Adrienne to continue and promise to return Dad's call later. Adrienne insists that I take the call in case something is wrong.

I walked in the bedroom and retrieved the phone from the purse just as the call was dropped. I called him back.

"Hey Dad, what is up?" I could hear Adrienne back in the kitchen and all I wanted to do was get back out on the balcony and finish our discussion.

"Hi honey. I just wanted to let you know that Laura and the family got off a few minutes ago."

"That is great Dad. Thanks for letting me know. Are you doing okay?"

"Oh yes, I am fine. I am kind of looking forward to some quiet time. I love everyone being here, but it has been a tiring week and I could use some rest. What are your girls up to?"

"We are on the balcony having coffee and catching up on things; just relaxing a bit ourselves." As I finished the last part of the sentence I was sure lightening was going to strike me down. Relaxed did not describe any part of the tension and nerves I was experiencing at the moment.

"Okay. I want you two to spend the day together. Do not worry about me. Go shopping, sit out by the pool, or do something that does not involve work or worry."

"I will let Adrienne know that you have given us those orders for the day Dad. She is standing right here." Adrienne had come in to my room to make sure everything was okay.

"Okay honey. Love you. Call me later."

"Okay Dad. Love you too".

"Is everything okay with Granddad?" Adrienne asked.

"Yes. As a matter of fact I think he wants some quiet time. He told us to spend the day together and not to worry about checking in on him."

"He is probably tired of all the company, not to mention all the stress of losing Grandma. It must be hard for him."

I led the way out of the bedroom and back to the balcony. "So where were we? In Miami I think."

"Yes, so anyway, this organization contacted me to inquire if I would be interested in working for them as a contracts attorney. A head-hunter working for their recruitment indicated that I had been recommended by one of my professors who has been doing some pro-bono work for them. It was weird though, because you would think that my contracts law professor, Dr. Whitman, would have contacted me first to see if I was interested in being recommended for the position."

"Adrienne, so far this sounds like an opportunity. What is up with it? Why were you worried to talk to me about it?"

"Mom, it is an opportunity. I just don't think you are going to like the job."

"Okay, what does that mean?"

"Children's NuDawn Organization is in the business of stopping trafficking of children for sex trade. My position would be to work with their existing legal to contract with safe houses and to deal with international issues arising from immigration, exportation and other complexities associated with their operations."

"Oh," I said as I looked closely at her. "Adrienne, this is honorable work. I am still not sure what you are not telling me."

"Well, the position would be based out of Miami, so that is good because it is closer to home, but the work would require me to travel and at times be in the thick of things. Meaning, I would travel some internationally, but I could also be at times in the middle of covert extractions which could hold some safety risks and I guess other issues."

I swallowed as I took in this information. As I looked at her, I could see the mixed emotion on her face.

"Adrienne, something must attract you to this offer. You are a bright, capable young woman who has many opportunities to grow with organizations. Why are you taking a second look at this?"

"Mom, at first I wasn't. I was shocked by the call from the recruiter. To be polite, I agreed to look over some documents and once I saw the statistics for these horrible crimes and circumstances, my gut just took over. I have been praying about this and I just don't have an answer yet. On the one hand, it sounds complicated and disturbing. On the other hand, it sounds captivating. I would be doing something that mattered for humans. I don't think it gets any more honorable than that."

"When do you have to give them an answer?"

"I told them I would let them know by next Friday. Something else that I didn't tell you because I didn't want to go in to it on the telephone; is that I flew down to Miami and interviewed with them two weeks ago. I am sorry I didn't tell you, but like I said, I thought we would have time to discuss it this weekend while I was home for Easter."

I reached over and put my hand on hers. I was at a loss for words. I didn't want to discourage her, but at the same time I was a little stunned by this development.

"Have you checked out this organization? Have they given you any references on their work? Who are their investors, that kind of due diligence on them?"

"Sort of, I guess. I did call Professor Whitman and talk with him. I also checked a couple of fraud sites to see if they had any claims or charges against them. I haven't asked them for references within their operations network but that is a good idea."

"You may also want to visit one of their safe houses. Talk with the staff. See how the process works on their end."

"Mom, I am sorry I didn't tell you before now. I should have known that you would be supportive and helpful. I was afraid you would think that I had lost my mind."

I half-jokingly replied, "Adrienne, I will always support you and your decisions. That may not always mean that you haven't lost your mind."

Smiling, she reached over and gave me a hug.

"Let's pray about this," I said. "God knows a whole lot more about this than we do and we need to lean on his direction."

As she and I bowed our heads and shared a prayer committed to seeking His guidance on this decision, I tried to focus on turning this over to His realm and opening our hearts to listen to His direction.

As we closed our prayer, I asked Adrienne how this would work with Andre if their relationship continued to grow.

"One more thing Mom, this is the interview that he is hoping goes his way. We are not competing for a job. He has interviewed for a different position within the organization. If he gets this job, and he should know this week, he will be moving to Miami."

"Wow! How did that happen?"

"Well, the co-worker that introduced us is really a potential future co-worker. Sorry for the small deception, but until I could tell you about the offer and organization, I had to change the details a bit. Andre and I met at a seminar put on by the recruitment agency to orient potential job candidates to the harsh reality of child trafficking. He and I were placed at a table together and we just hit it off immediately."

"Adrienne, at this point am I missing any more of the story? I am getting a bit overwhelmed at the stream of new information."

"Sorry Mom. No, you are up to speed now. That is all the details. What do you think about the offer Mom?"

"Honey I don't know yet. I am going to do some research on my own and I would like to ask you to reach out to your key contact there and see if there is a possibility to check out one of the safe houses. Florida would be nice, but other places are a possibility. I think you will feel better about having that information to make your decision."

"I love you Mom. Thanks for helping me with this."

"You are welcome. That is one of my many jobs."

As we finished up on the balcony, Adrienne went to her room to get the contact information and make the necessary calls. I retrieved my laptop from my bedroom. I need to better understand this organization, their mission, their outreach, and most of all whether they are a safe and reputable place for my daughter to work.

CHAPTER 23 ▬▬▬▬▬▬▬▬▬

Adrienne and I spent the next couple of hours researching Children's NuDawn; their work, their reputation, and other organizations that are providing similar outreach. One thing is clear. This organization seems to be on the forefront of both the prevention of child trafficking as well as the interception and safe rescue of children who are victims of this horrendous abuse.

Adrienne spoke with her contact at NuDawn and he had offered several options as references for safe houses within one hundred miles of our home.

"Mom, if you want to go with me, the intervention specialist that I spoke with in Tampa has offered Friday as an option for coming to visit the facility."

"I would like that Adrienne. I think it is important, especially with your commitment to make this decision on whether you want to go through with this job opportunity."

Adrienne left to go make the arrangements for Friday and I sat down on the couch. As I thought about the implications of this type of work, I felt a huge weight on my chest. Our shy, conservative, serious girl could be leaving a safe, secure, career booster position to become involved with the dark side of child abuse. On the one hand, I understood her attraction to this offer. It could be a ministry of sorts, a way to put her education and expertise to work in saving God's children. The other side of me, the mother; worried that she would see things, experience things and operate in a world that could change someone. Change the innocence. Change the disposition. Sour a perspective.

As I continue with my thoughts, Adrienne returns to the living room to let me know that we are scheduled for a meeting at 10:00 on Friday. Given the security of the safe house, we will be met at a designated place by one of the house staff and then transported to the location by the staff member to ensure that we are not followed.

I look at Adrienne closely. I see a fire in her eyes that I have not seen before. *Is it possible that this may be her passion?*

The words to the well-known children's song; "Jesus loves the little children, all the children of the world" began to play in my head. This may be her calling, a place where she can contribute in such an important way.

"Okay honey. We will be there. I am looking forward to it."

As I walk in the kitchen to put my coffee cup away and wash the pot, I suggest that we go have some fun, get out of the house. Maybe some shopping is in order.

"Adrienne, let's hit the boutiques on the island. Does that sound like a plan?"

"Yes Mom. I would love to do that."

"I will get a shower and change. I think lunch on the avenue, outside under the umbrellas, would be a great way to get started. We will be hungry by then."

Within a half hour, we were both dressed and ready to leave when my cell phone rang. For a second my thoughts went to *something must be wrong with Mother.* Then I realized of course, mother isn't here anymore.

"Hello?"

"Hi Becky, this is Anne from Hospice. Did I catch you at a bad time?"

"Oh no Anne, it is good to hear from you. How can I help you?"

"Well, first I wanted to know how the family is doing. I really enjoyed meeting all of you and really admired the way that your family supports each other.

"Anne, we are doing fine. It is taking some adjustment, but I know that our mother is in a better place."

"It will take time to heal and adjust."

"Thank you for your concern. We appreciate all of your help through the end days with Mother."

"I am glad that we were helpful. The other reason that I called is to let you know about another family that is going through a similar time. The mother is currently in the hospital and the father is beside himself. He is finding it difficult to manage without his wife and the grown children are struggling as well. I know you have just had a huge emotional toll with the passing of your mother, but there is something about you and your situation that I think would be beneficial to the husband and his children. You have a gift Becky. A gift of feeling the emotion, and experience that is invaluable in coping with this disease."

"Well, that is kind of you Anne. I don't know what to say. What is it exactly that you need my help to do?"

"One of the daughters, Deidre, was in the waiting room the day your mother died. I was in there with some of your family members, as well as your pastor and his wife. Deidre noticed the love and support of your family and it made a real impression on her. She has asked if someone from your family would be willing to talk to them. She knows that you have lost your mother and the timing is an issue, but I promised her I would ask you. She wants to understand how to get through this and especially how to pull her family together. Becky, you can say no. You are still in the grief process. But I am hoping you will say yes."

"How far along in the disease process is the mother? I am assuming that since you are involved through hospice, that she doesn't have much time."

"Realistically, as you know, we never know. But I don't think she is at the end stage yet, maybe a week or two, but then again, maybe not."

"Anne, I would love to help but I have a few things on my plate right now. Would you mind if I pray about it and discuss it with my girls and then get back to you?"

"Not at all Becky, I completely understand."

"Okay then. I will call you tomorrow."

"Thanks again, Becky, and my regards to your family."

As I hung up the telephone, I felt both exhausted at all of the things going on, yet somehow motivated to help this family. My first priority though is Adrienne. As we left to go shopping, I reminded myself to be in the 'present' for her. She needs my time and I need her.

Chapter 24

Adrienne and I were having a lunch of salads and fresh baked sourdough bread when Collette called. I had been meaning to call her to thank her for the chicken casserole she had brought over to Dad's yesterday, but just hadn't had a chance to make that call.

"Hey Collette, how are you doing?"

"I am doing fabulous, but I am really calling to check and see how all of you were doing."

I briefed her on Laura and her family's departure earlier in the day and continued with Amelia at work and Dad at home resting up from all of the company. I finished with Adrienne and my lunching on Island Avenue.

"That sounds great," Collette said. "I am glad that you two are getting some time alone. Is there anything that I can do for you?"

"No, I think we are all doing as well as you would expect given the circumstances. I plan to give Dad a call a little later and see if I can convince him to come over to my place for dinner. He may not be up to it but the change of scenery would do him good."

"Well, I know that Russell is planning to stop by there and see him on his way home from the church office today. Is there anything that you can think of that Russell can do?"

"Not that I can think of right now, Collette. Thank you for asking. I may want to ring you up in a day or so and talk through some things with you. What are you doing tomorrow?"

"I am pretty open. We have our prayer circle tomorrow night at the church, but other than that I am available. Just let me know when you want to get together."

"I will. And thank you for everything. The chicken casserole was delicious and I know everyone was so appreciative of you taking the time to make that and helping with the church ladies food preparation on Saturday. You are a true friend."

"I wish I could have done more, but you are more than welcome. Now finish your lunch with Adrienne, tell her I said hello, and call me when you want to get together."

"Ok, and thanks again."

As Adrienne and I finished our lunch, I thought about how much I would value Collette's opinion on both the NuDawn job option for Adrienne and the request of Anne to speak with the family. Maybe Collette would go with me. I would have to think about it some more.

Shopping proved to be therapeutic and expensive. Adrienne found two dresses that she loved and that complimented her shape and features beautifully. One of the dresses we purchased with the thought of her wearing it to Amelia's rehearsal dinner. The dress has a pale yellow background with honey-gold swirl print over the entire dress. It is sleeveless and form fitting, without being too tight. She found shoes in a non-metallic gold that match the dress perfectly. The high heels put her a little over six feet tall, but she said she loved being tall. She concluded with a comment about Andre being six foot three inches tall.

Clearly she is still thinking about inviting him to the wedding. I find myself hoping that she does. I would like to meet him and get a feel for his interest and attraction to NuDawn.

I also shopped, finding a beautiful pants and tunic set in off-white. I purchased a lilac silk chemise to go under the outfit and a pair of pearlized mule style shoes with a stacked heel. The ensemble is very chic and with the upcoming wedding and still one more wedding shower, I am sure I will find an occasion to wear it.

Arms and hands full of shopping bags, we head back to the car. As we pass by a coffee shop, we both decide that a hot tea on the outside deck would be a perfect way to end this excursion. After dropping the shopping bags in the car a block down, we both walk back to the coffee shop and find a seat with a view of the street. Watching the shop patrons walk the streets while sipping triple-berry tea proved to be entertaining and relaxing.

"Mom, can you believe that car? Wow."

"That is one fancy car."

"Do you know how much those cars cost? It must be serious money."

"Well, several years ago, one of your Dad and I's partners purchased one. I think his was well over $100,000."

"Seriously? Someone would pay that for a car and then park it on the street to get the doors dinged?"

"Cars and status are important to some people, but I agree, this one is over the top."

As we finished admiring and talking about the expense of the car, a gentleman in his mid-fifties or so walked up to the car, opened the door and then climbed in.

"Adrienne, I know that gentleman. He is one of the owners of the local television stations. He is frequently airing his opinions on political matters."

"He is handsome Mom. And he has a *really* nice car," she said smiling at me and clearly trying to get a rise out of me. I decide to play her game.

"Well Adrienne, you know what they say. First time love, second time money. Maybe I will just go out and find me a really, really rich guy and shack up with him."

"Mom, don't even say that!" As she says that she looks up at the sky, "Dad, she didn't mean it. Grandma, she didn't mean it." As she rolls her eyes at me I reply with a huge grin. Maybe she will stop trying to set me up for a while.

As she continued to playfully glare at me, I sent up my own quiet apology to Roger. Hopefully he knew that was a joke.

Pulling out from the parking space and in to the Island Avenue traffic, my cell phone is playing Dad's ring.

"Hello Dad. How are you doing?"

"Great, honey. I am just checking on your girls. Are you having a great day?"

"We are! We have just finished some shopping and we're headed back to my place. Can we lure you in to coming over, having some dinner and watching the sunset with us?"

"Well I don't know. We still have all of this food here. Maybe I could bring it over and get it out of my refrigerator. I will never eat all of this stuff."

"Dad, don't worry about that. Adrienne and I will come over tomorrow and repackage things and bring home what you don't want. I thought I would fix some of Adrienne's favorites tonight. You know I don't get to cook much for her anymore."

As I glanced over at her she was smiling and doing an exaggerated clap.

"Maybe I can even get Amelia and Craig over. I think I will make shrimp scampi with salad and garlic rolls. How does that sound?"

"It sounds good and I think I would like to do that. I am kind of tired of being cooped up in the house. What time do you want me to come over?"

I glanced at my watch and saw that it was already 4:30.

"What about 6:00 o'clock, Dad? That will give us some time to stop by the seafood market and then get home."

"That sounds good. Can I bring anything? What about this coconut cake that the neighbor's brought over. It hasn't even been sliced yet."

"That would be great Dad. That is one of Adrienne's favorites. We will see you at 6:00!"

"Now that is exciting," I said to Adrienne after finishing the call. "Getting Dad out of the house and hanging out for the sunset is good medicine."

Adrienne nodded in agreement and we headed to the market.

"Text Amelia and let her know our plan. She doesn't get off until between six and seven o'clock, but she may want to meet Craig at our place for dinner. We will buy enough of everything, just in case they decide to come."

As Adrienne finished texting, I turned in to Bay Seafood's parking lot and found a space. Quaint, but always busy, this is our favorite spot for the freshest seafood in the area.

Amelia texted back to Adrienne and said she would run the dinner invitation by Craig. He is scheduled to fly out tomorrow for a few days so she isn't sure he will be up for it, but she will let us know. At the very least, she will come by and visit us on her way home.

Adrienne and I finish with our purchases and return to the condo. One good thing about seafood dinners is they are easy to prepare and quick on time. I began peeling and butterflying the shrimp and Adrienne started the salad. As I work with the shrimp, I decide that we have time to roast the garlic in preparation for the scampi sauce and I prep the garlic in olive oil in a small pan and place it in the oven. Roasted garlic pulverized adds so much depth and flavor to the scampi sauce, rather than just sautéing the garlic.

As we work in the kitchen together, I think about all that has transpired in the past week. Just one week ago today, Mom was taken to the hospital. It is impossible to think about how many things have gone on in the last seven days. The emotions, the decisions, the exhaustion, and yet one week later I am in my kitchen, cooking with my daughter, after a day of shopping and spending good quality time with her.

I think about how blessed I am to have this time and how resilient we are in God's grace. Knowing my mother is spending this very night in God's kingdom is the only way that I can fathom the release from grief at her loss and the ability to find joy in the events of today. I wish Mom could have enjoyed these kinds of nights with us. She missed so much by becoming sick at such a young age. She would have loved the girls and the fine women that they have become. With that last thought, tears welled up and I had to step away from the kitchen and in to the bathroom. Tears at what might have been will dampen the joy of the present and I want to cherish every moment.

As I make my way back to the kitchen, I realize that Adrienne hasn't missed my quick exit, or the likely reason for my sudden departure.

"Mom, are you okay?"

"Yes honey, I am fine. Just finishing up with the shrimp, do you need me to help you with the salad?"

"Mom, you don't always have to be strong. You lost your mother. If you need to cry or be by yourself, you should take that time."

The tears so close to the emotional surface rise again. I turn around and look at Adrienne. "Adrienne, thank you for saying that, and I am sure you mean what you say. I will grieve for Mom, probably many days over the next years. But tonight I want to be present here, with you and your grandfather. Looking back if we need to, but also healing and moving forward. We are not guaranteed tomorrow, and so today matters."

Adrienne eyes brim and tears slip down both cheeks. "Mom, you are so amazing. You are *always* saying and doing the right thing. But if you are sad, if we are sad, then we need to let it out. Then we can get past it and move forward. I don't think you can fast-forward grief."

"Honey," I said as I put my arms around her. "I want you to process your grandmother's death in whatever way you need to. If you need to cry, cry. If you need to reminisce, reminisce. Whatever you need, I am here for you. And I will do the same."

With the dinner preparations mostly complete, we each go to our rooms to freshen up before Dad arrives. As I stand in my bathroom reapplying some make-up, I ask God to help me be there for my daughters and Dad. "Lord, you know what each of us needs right now. Put your arms around us and comfort us. Give us the strength and patience to move forward in faith, mending our hearts and growing in your precious love, Amen."

As I came out of the bedroom and in to the living room, Adrienne was already relaxing on the couch.

"Mom, I don't want to say anything yet to granddad or Amelia about the job offer."

"Okay, that is fine, any particular reason?"

"Well, it may not pan out and I would rather spend the time tonight being together. It is a beautiful day, there will be a beautiful sunset, and I just want everyone to relax. Talking about human trafficking probably won't facilitate relaxation." Adrienne smiled slightly at her last sentence.

"That is your call. I am sure your grandfather and Amelia both would be supportive, but I will keep quiet about it for now if that is what you want."

"I think it is better."

The doorbell rang and Dad came in, carrying the coconut cake. He also had one of the vases of flowers from the house in his hand.

"Dad, the flowers are beautiful. Thank you for thinking of bringing them over," I said.

"Well, I knew you girls would enjoy them and I thought these were the prettiest of the ones that came in the last two days. Your mother would have loved them, with all of the baby's breath and pink roses. Those were some of her favorites."

Adrienne hugged her grandfather and invited him out on the balcony. The table was set to eat out there and the weather was perfect. In another forty-five minutes or so the sun would set. I grabbed some snacks and a chilled bottle of white wine and headed out to sit with them. Amelia had texted and said that she would stop by on the way home and Craig would meet her here. As I poured the wine, I found myself looking forward to the evening. Hopefully, as a family, we could lean on each other and begin to transition in to the next phase of our lives; a big hill to climb considering we had been in a caretaker role for so many years.

I sat back as Adrienne filled her grandfather in on her work, her life in Charlotte and her hopes and dreams. Dad listened intently. He has always been the Dad that listened and wanted to be part of his children's lives. That has always included not only his children, but his grandchildren as well.

As Adrienne talked about her dreams and plans, I noticed that she carefully left out the immediate opportunity. Instead, she skirted the details by telling her grandfather that she wanted to do something "that matters" with her life. I have a feeling that the job offer, and the business it represents, is taking root in her heart.

"Hello!" Amelia called. She and Craig were both walking through the living room and out to the balcony.

"Hi! I am so glad you could make it. Craig, it is good to see you. Come on in and sit down. We are just talking and enjoying the pre-sunset," I said.

"Mom, this is a great idea. All I have been able to think about for the last hour of work is watching the sun set and eating scampi!"

"Good because that is exactly the plan".

Craig pulled out the chair for Amelia and then sat down in the chair between Adrienne and Amelia. He looked handsome this evening, in a pale blue corduroy shirt and faded jeans. Brown loafers and flight glasses on a cord around his neck completed his look.

Always polite, and clearly crazy about Amelia, he will be a good husband and father, should they have children someday. Although I occasionally react to his inflated ego, he is a good man and he is good for Amelia. I have thanked God many times for finding a man of his caliber for my daughter to love and with whom she will spend the rest of her life.

As the conversation continued and the time flew by, the sun began to set. I grabbed my camera and took pictures of the family, sun setting in the background of a near perfect day.

Dinner was served and everyone raved about their meal. It was good to see Dad enjoy himself, without having to skip the meal or shorten the stay to go be with Mom. He loved every minute of taking care of her, but it had taken its toll. I love him for his devotion, but I sincerely hope that he can find new purpose in the coming months. Mom's care has been such a big part of his life that it could be difficult for him to make the transition.

As we cut the coconut cake, we tease Craig and Amelia about 'practicing' feeding the cake to each other in anticipation of their wedding in just a few short weeks. Amelia is threatening to make Craig wear the cake and he is taunting her with how sweet she needs to be over the next few weeks or else; meaning she would be wearing the cake.

Dad was the first to depart looking a bit tired but relaxed. I sensed that he was also a little emotional but that was to be expected. Amelia and Craig left just after Dad.

Amelia works tomorrow and Friday, but will be off Saturday and Sunday. Craig will leave tomorrow and be back on Sunday. Given their schedules, there is a good chance that Amelia, Adrienne and I can spend Saturday together. I hope so. There are still a few wedding details to attend to and it would be nice to spend time with just the three of us.

As Adrienne and I clean the kitchen, Adrienne chats about Craig and Amelia.

"They seem so good together Mom. I am happy for them. You would think two very independent people with busy careers and all would be only in to themselves, but both of them are clearly in to each other. I hope I can find someone like that."

"You will honey. Don't settle for anything less. I know Amelia adores Craig, and although she has her busy career and he is gone a lot, they work to focus on each other when they are together. As long as they continue to work at it, they will have a good life together. I am very happy for both of them and excited about the wedding."

"It will be great to have a brother. I really like Craig."

THE THURSDAY
AFTER EASTER

CHAPTER 25

I awoke at 6:00 am and padded into the kitchen in my slippers. Adrienne's room door was closed and I couldn't hear any sounds coming from her room. Hopefully she is getting some well-deserved rest. As I start the coffee, I think about the day ahead. I want to spend most of the day with Adrienne but there are some things at the office that I need to handle. I have been copied on the emails from the office and I know that they are managing things to give me the time that I need with my family. Thoughtful of them, and yet I also know that some of the items on the docket for this week need my attention. I will brew the coffee, get a shower and if Adrienne is still asleep, leave her a note and let her know that I will be at the office for a couple of hours.

Just as I am putting the final touches on my make-up, I hear Adrienne call at the bedroom door.

"Come in honey, I am getting dressed. Did you sleep well?"

"Yes, I slept like a log. Are you going somewhere?"

"Yes, I thought I would go in to the office for a couple of hours and catch up on a few things. Why don't you relax here and I will try to be back by 10:00 or so. Then we will have the day to spend however you would like."

"Okay. That sounds good. Maybe I will go for a walk on the beach and then come back and get a shower."

"Perfect." I pick up my sweater and purse and we both walk to the kitchen.

"If you want some breakfast there is yogurt in the refrigerator and cereal in the pantry. I promised your Grandfather that we would come over sometime today and deal with the food in his refrigerator. Maybe we can do that when I get back."

"Plus that will give us a chance to spend some time with Granddad. Have you heard from him this morning?"

"No. He is probably hoping that we are sleeping in late. I will give him a call on my way to the office."

"Okay Mom, see you in a little while."

As I walk down the stairs to my car I notice the chill in the air. This is likely one of the last weeks of spring before the warmer days begin. I love this time of year and will miss these cool mornings as summer approaches and the Florida heat builds up for the very hot days of June, July and August.

As I drove south on Gulf Drive, I dialed Dad's number. After several rings, the call went to voice mail.

"Hi Dad, I am just checking on you. Give me a call when you have a few minutes. I am going to the office for a couple of hours and then Adrienne and I will be over your way to visit."

As I near the office, I think about additional research that I want to do on the NuDawn Organization and the topic of human trafficking. Tomorrow, Adrienne and I will travel to Tampa to see some of how the operation works but I want to be prepared to ask good questions and keep an eye out for anything that seems off; not right.

As I park the car my cell phone is ringing. Expecting Dad's return call, the caller ID shows Amelia.

"Good morning Amelia."

"Hi Mom. I just called to see what you and Adrienne are planning to do today."

"Well, I am just getting to the office to catch up on a few things. Adrienne is up and she is going to go for a walk on the beach. Then she and I are going over to Dad's to clean out the refrigerator and deal with all of the food that is left over. After that, who knows what we will find to do."

"That sounds like a good day. I think Craig and I are going to spend some time together tonight. We haven't seen much of each other and his trip for today is postponed until tomorrow."

"I think that is a good idea. You both have a lot to take care of, with the wedding right around the corner."

"Okay, well I better get out on the floor and see what the ER holds for me today. Love you Mom."

"Love you too honey, good-bye".

I unlock the back door of the office, noticing that there is one other car in the parking garage; Mary's. I am not surprised that she is here at 7:15 in the morning; especially with the number of days that I have been out of the office. My absence increases her workload. I will have to do something special for her in the coming week, maybe an extra day off once things settle back to normal.

"Good morning Mary."

Mary turned around with a surprised look on her face. "Hello Mrs. Kennedy. I didn't know that you were planning on coming in today." Despite the fact that Mary has worked for me for years, she still addresses me formally in the office. On the rare occasion that we are out socially at a gathering or event, she might call me Becky, but never in the office.

"I am just in for a little while Mary. Adrienne and I are going to spend the next few days together before she goes back to Charlotte. I have been able to keep up with your emails and I know that the filing documents are going out today on the Arnold case. I also want to check in on the suit filed with Sampson & Company."

The Arnold case is all set. Doug Andrews finalized the papers yesterday and they were sent out by courier last night. They should receive them today," Mary explained. "On the suit with Sampson & Company, we did hear back from the court late yesterday that an initial hearing has been set for May 10th. Judge Smith will be the presiding judge, which should be good for us."

"Yes, that will be good," I commented. Judge Smith is known as an objective and fair judge. Dealing with the facts of the case head-on is the best way to operate in his court and the kind of hearing I like best.

"Anything else going on that I need to know?"

"We picked up two new cases this week. One Doug Andrews took and the other Kathryn is handling." Kathryn Sawyer was the newest member of my law team and she was proving to be a great addition to the firm.

"Great. What type of cases?"

"Doug's is a straight foreclosure. The one Kathryn is working is a little more complicated. The family has always been faithful about paying the mortgage on the home but the father was recently in a serious auto accident and has been out of work for four months. The mortgage insurance that the family purchased has a sixty day out of work waiting period in the policy. The insurance company is refusing to pay, citing that the policy is exempt from payment if the loss is due to negligence. The insured was cited in the accident with drunk driving. The family is suing the insurance company for policy coverage, since the policy language does not specifically address drunk driving and therefore the definition of negligence is challenged. In the meantime, the bank has sent a notice to begin foreclosure if the mortgage arrears are not paid by the first of the month."

"Okay, that is a complicated one. Has Kathryn been in touch with the bank's counsel?"

"I am not sure. I can have her send you an email when she comes in."

"I will be here when she comes in unless she is delayed for some reason this morning. I thought I would work for a couple of hours. Let me know when she gets in".

"I will, Mrs. Kennedy."

As I sat down at my desk, I opened my telephone message inbox. At the firm, all telephone messages are logged in an electronic format on the office intranet. This method allows for any of the staff or attorneys to follow up on any of the cases if there is an emergency. All of the case records are electronic and a call record is maintained on each case.

As I scroll through the messages, I see a total of four messages from Matthew Green. *What am I going to do about this guy?*

The first two messages from Matthew were condolences. The first was taken by Mary and the other by Stephanie Cox, the office receptionist. The third message requested a call back, taken by Stephanie and the fourth was left yesterday with Mary asking for a return call. No subject matter or call purpose listed for calls three and four. I ignore the request for a return call and peruse through the other messages. Most are condolences from other law firm representatives, a few from individuals at the courthouse and several from real estate firms that I deal with as part of my practice. One call stood out. John Stillman had left a message. That seemed odd and reminded me that I still owed Anne a response about speaking with the family at the hospital.

I pick up the telephone and dial the number to the Hospice office. At 7:45 in the morning, I will most likely get his voice mail. I assume he is calling to follow up on Anne's request but that seems to me to be a level of detail that would be outside the administrative attention of the organization's Director.

On the third ring, John answers. "Hello, this is John Stillman."

Surprised that he is at his desk I reply, "Hello John, this is Becky Kennedy. I am in the office this morning and see from my message that you called yesterday. How can I help you?"

"Good morning Becky. Thank you for returning my call. I was speaking with Anne yesterday and she shared with me her request for you to consider speaking with the Carter family."

"Yes, well Anne didn't mention their last name but she did make the request. I guess their daughter, Deidre, was in the waiting room while our family was there."

"That is right. Becky, Anne and I discussed the unusual nature of this request. We normally do not make these types of requests, or involve grieving families in our outreach. I was a little surprised that Anne called you about this and I want to make sure that you know we will understand if you are in any way uncomfortable."

"I appreciate you taking the time to call me. Anne was considerate in her request and did not place any pressure on my decision. I did ask her to give me some time to think about it."

"Well, I understand that and again Becky, please know that we completely understand if you decide that it is too much for you right now."

"Thanks again John. I don't feel that it is too much to ask and I will give Anne a call later today with my decision."

"Okay Becky. That sounds good. Also, if you decide to meet with the family and want one of us to accompany you, we would be happy to do that. It may make it easier and a smoother introduction to the family."

"Thank you John. I will speak with you soon."

"Good-bye and thanks again Becky."

"Good-bye." As I ended the call, I had mixed emotions. I knew I would most likely meet with the family, but I still felt kind of odd about the request.

I spent another hour looking through documents that had piled in my inbox and other mail. Mary buzzed me that Kathryn had arrived and I asked her to have Kathryn come in when she gets settled. Just as I was finishing the last of the mail Kathryn walked in.

"Hello Becky, how are you?"

"I am doing fine, Kathryn. Thank you for asking."

"How is your Dad holding up?"

"I think he is doing very well considering everything. The next few weeks will tell more about how he adjusts, but for now I would say he is doing well."

"The funeral was lovely Becky. What a tribute to your mother and her incredible legacy."

"Thanks Kathryn. I appreciate that. I just wanted to touch base with you on this new case."

"Yes, the Mendoza case." As Kathryn walked through the details of the case, I asked a few questions about the policy and her early findings in speaking with the bank. Clearly she was covering the necessary bases and her forward strategy was well thought out and her sense of urgency in resolving some of the immediate questions clear.

"Sounds like you have the initial bases covered. Keep me posted if you don't mind".

"I will Becky. Any additional thoughts or insight that you have as we go forward is appreciated."

"You got it Kathryn. Thanks for the good work."

As Kathryn left the office I picked up the work notes that I had made for Mary and walked to her desk. Doug was coming in the door and we stopped to chat for a few minutes. He updated me on several of the cases that he was handling for me and everything seemed to be going fairly smoothly.

Mary and I were reviewing my notes when I heard the chime of the office front door. Mary excused herself saying that Stephanie will not be in until 9:00 this morning. As I stood at Mary's desk, she returned holding a vase of yellow roses.

"Those are beautiful Mary. Who sent them?"

Mary opened the card and frowned slightly and then smiled.

"I am not sure I should have opened the card Mrs. Kennedy. I think it is intended for you to open."

"What?" I asked as I took the card from her and opened to the message.

The card read:

Becky, I hope these yellow roses bring some cheer to your day. I am thinking of you in your time of loss. Love Matthew.

I looked at Mary and put my hands out palms up.

"What in the world is that," I asked, "a condolence or a love note?"

"I think the latter," Mary said; "disguised as a condolence. Has he called you lately?"

"Yes, he called the other night but I didn't take his call, I let it go to voice mail."

"When was that?"

"The night I picked Adrienne up, so that would have been Friday night. I had just picked her up at the airport and we were headed to the hospital. It wasn't a good time to have a conversation with him."

"Well, Mrs. Kennedy, you know what he wants. At some point I guess you will have to deal with him one way or the other."

I rolled my eyes as I let out a sigh. "I guess I will. I have no intention of going out with him. I guess the sooner I tell him the better for all of us."

As I said good-bye to Mary and left the office I knew that a call to Matthew Green was next on my list.

I sat in the SUV in the parking garage and dialed Matthew Green's office number. The receptionist indicated that he was in the office and put me through to his extension.

"Becky, it is nice to hear from you!"

"Good morning Matthew. I was just in the office and received the roses that you sent over. Thank you, that was thoughtful of you."

"It is my pleasure Becky. I just want you to know that I have been thinking of you. I saw your car pull in the garage this morning on my way to work so I figured you are back in the office and may need something cheerful to look at while you work."

Why did I have the weird feeling that he was watching me or something? Shake it off Becky, I coached myself.

"Well, again Matthew, that is very thoughtful of you."

"So, are you back at work now?"

"Not yet. My youngest daughter is still in town and I will be spending some time with her before she returns home." For some reason, I felt the need to be vague; youngest daughter, instead of calling her by name, returns home, instead of heads back to Charlotte. *What was my issue? Why did I feel that I needed to protect my privacy with this guy?*

"Oh, I see; so Monday then?"

"Yes, Monday."

"I would like to take you to lunch once you are back. What day would work best for you next week?"

"Matthew, I appreciate your friendship but I am not interested in anything beyond that. I don't think lunch is a good idea right now."

"Becky, it is lunch. You have to eat. I admit that I would like for it to become more than that, but if friends is where it needs to be, then that is where it will stay." Matthew's tone was slightly edgy; no doubt a guy that wasn't accustomed to being deterred. Still my gut was in full caution mode.

"Matthew, I appreciate your understanding. Let me get back in the swing of things and then we can go from there."

"I understand, Becky. This has been a tough few weeks for you. Let me know if there is anything that I can do for you. Take care."

"Thanks Matthew, you too."

As I end the call I feel tired. Dealing with a social life takes energy and motivation. I have neither right now for that. And even if I did, Matthew Green is not the guy.

My next call is to Collette. I am hoping that she has time for a cup of coffee before I head back to the condo. I want to talk to her about the request from Anne and get her two cents on the NuDawn deal.

"Hi Collette, it is Becky."

"Hi Becky, I was hoping that I would hear from you today. What are you and Adrienne up to this morning?"

"Actually, Adrienne is back at the condo. I came in to the office for a little while to catch up on a few things. I am wondering if you have time for a cup of coffee and some much needed guidance for a friend."

"Of course I do. I am just off to the grocery store but I will meet you instead. How about the Coffee Café? Will that work?"

"Yes, that is perfect." I looked at my watch. "Does 9:15 give you enough time to get here?

"It will. I should be there in five minutes or so."

I decide to walk rather than drive the two blocks to the cafe. Just as I turn the corner to enter the café I see Collette parking her van. I wave and smile as she crosses the street.

Inside Collette listens patiently as I share my conversation with Anne and then John Stillman. "Well, what do you think?" I asked.

"Well Becky, it is up to you. But I understand why they would ask. As a pastor's wife, involved with Russell in family ministry, the family that has the eternal view of death is rare. Even among Christians, the terminal illness and certainty of death is difficult. We live in the here and now and most of the time our natural thoughts center on life without the person and the resulting complexities of day to day issues. Rarely, except in long term illness, do we see the family who is focused on the joy of entering God's Kingdom. It is just human nature. Because of your faith, and likely your past experience with Roger's death, you have a view that is grounded in the certainty of heaven. Most families just aren't there. And, if they are not Christians, they are most likely dealing with the finality of death which is even more difficult."

I thought about that for a few minutes. I knew that what Collette said was true, but I also knew that Mother's long term illness was the biggest component. When Roger died, although I have an eternal view as a Christian, that view was not my focus at his unexpected death. I *was* the person trying to cope with how to wake up the next day and put one foot in front of the other. I realized as I thought about Collette's observations that I have been in both of the scenarios. I have had the experience of an unexpected loss and a long term illness death. Both Roger and Mother are in heaven, of that I am sure, but how I cope and eventually recover are very different.

"Collette, that is helpful. You are in the day to day thick of dealing with families and their losses. I realize that I understand both. I have been the widow that has worried about how to get through the day without Roger and I have been the daughter and a care-giver for decades who sees God's Kingdom as the reward my Mother deserves that will take her away from her suffering."

"Becky, if you would like for me to go with you to talk to this family, I would be happy to and I know Russell would go as well if you think that would be of benefit to them."

"Collette, thank you, that means so much but I think what I may do is have either Anne or John go with me. I would like to offer to the family the option to meet with you and Russell if they show an interest. Would that be ok?"

"Absolutely, we would be happy to talk with them."

"Okay, good. Now, on to what may be the tougher topic for the day."

"Uh oh, what's up?"

As I launched in to the NuDawn opportunity of Adrienne's, Collette listened intently occasionally drawing imaginary lines on the table with her finger. When I finished the overview and the brief information that I had from my research, I paused for her reaction.

"This is really an interesting potential change of path for Adrienne. I am not familiar with this group but I am generally familiar with some of the mission work that has been done by churches and various ministries to try and fund some of the efforts like these. The problem is a big one and I think the interventions are important work. I know it is a little scary for you and likely for Adrienne. What can I do to help?"

"Well, I mostly just want an ear and you are my best friend. I don't know enough about it to even ask the right questions."

"Researching it is certainly a step in the right direction and the fact that you and Adrienne will be getting a chance to look first hand at some of the operation and ask questions is a really great idea. Would you like me to ask Russell if he is familiar with this group and get any feedback that he may have on the topic? He is obviously a lot more connected to any day to day information than I am and he can also research some of his Christian periodicals for additional information."

"Collette that would be awesome. If he has the time I would really appreciate his input. And frankly, although Adrienne doesn't know I am here talking to you about it, I think that any thumbs up Russell could give to the reputation of this group would be appreciated by her as well."

"Consider it done then. I will stop by his office on the way to the grocery store and we will catch up with you by telephone before your trip tomorrow."

"You are such a good friend. Thank you."

As we made our way out of the coffee shop, I was grateful for Collette's friendship. I felt like she was a kindred spirit of sorts, always keen on what I needed at the moment and always willing to dig in where needed. I hoped she would always feel that commitment from me as well. I looked at my watch and saw that it was five minutes before 10:00. It was time to get back to Adrienne and then to Dad's. I watched Collette drive away and then went back in to the café. I ordered Adrienne's favorite, a bear claw cinnamon pastry to go with the next pot of coffee I would make as soon as I got home.

CHAPTER 26

As I walked back to the car from the café, it occurred to me that Dad had not returned my phone call. That was a little odd. I reached for my cell phone and redialed his number. The message went to voice mail again. As I left a second message and tried to sound casual, my heart was in my throat. *Where was he?* Dad had carried his cell phone everywhere with him for the last twenty years, always on alert for a call about Mother. Surely he couldn't have pitched that habit in a few days.

As I climbed in to the SUV I decided to detour by Dad's on the way back to my condo. Just a few miles out of the way, I knew I would feel better and could relax with Adrienne if I was reassured that he was okay.

I drove the short distance to Dad's and as I turned onto his street from the main highway I saw his truck turning in to his driveway. He hadn't spotted my vehicle yet and it occurred to me that I could turn around and he wouldn't know I was checking up on him, but curiosity won out and I parked behind his car in the driveway.

"Hi Dad," I said as I lowered the window and leaned out.

"Hi honey. I didn't expect to see you here so early."

"Well, technically I am only here for a second. I went to the office for a few hours this morning and now I am going back home to hang out with Adrienne for a while. I came by because I called you a couple of times and got your voice mail, which is unusual so

I just wanted to stop by and see if you were okay." Even to me as I explained my impromptu stop, it sounded lame.

"Oh Becky, everything is fine. I decided to go to the corner restaurant for breakfast and I forgot to charge my cell phone last night. The battery is dead."

"Ok. Well I just wanted to check on you. Since you always have your cell with you I wasn't sure what to make of it."

"Well that is understandable. I am sorry if I made you worry but everything is fine here."

"Okay Dad. Adrienne and I will be over later to clean out the refrigerator and visit with you. What time would work best for you?"

"Anytime honey. The only plan I have is to mow the yard and I am going to get started on that right now."

"Alright then, I would guess that we will probably come over early to mid-afternoon. See you then." I gave Dad another hug and backed out of the driveway. As I drove away I thought about how worried I had been and realized that my gut is still in the worry zone with him. I need to do my best to reel it in. I don't want to give Dad the impression that I am hovering. He needs my love, but he also needs some space. Note to self; don't over-react.

Adrienne was dressed and ready when I got home. As I started to make another pot of coffee, she spied her treat from the café.

"Mom, tell me that you did not bring me a bear claw from the café."

"Actually Adrienne, I forgot to get you one. That one is for me."

"It is not," she said as she grabbed the bakery bag from the counter.

I smiled and tried to grab it away from her. She playfully hid it behind her back and side-stepped my reach. We both started laughing and she did a victory win gesture with both arms in the air. Of course, the huge pastry probably weighs a pound and the reality is she would never finish it. But the light-hearted banter was good fun.

Adrienne took her pastry and we both fixed a cup of coffee and went out to the balcony. Although it had warmed up significantly since the early morning, it was still quite pleasant. The beach was getting more crowded as the day wore on, but still much less crowded than the weekend crush of sun-bathers and families over the Easter weekend.

"I talked with Andre this morning," Adrienne offered. "I told him about our conversation and the planned visit tomorrow. He thought it was a great idea and wished he was here to join us."

"That would be good but I guess a quick flight to Florida is out of the question," I said.

"Yes, he won't be able to come but he did say that he will want to hear everything about it when we get back."

"Did he have any questions about the program that he wants us to ask while we are there?"

"I didn't really ask him that Mom, but I should. I will call him again later."

I knew I should fess up and let Adrienne know that I had confided in Collette.

"I spoke with Collette about it this morning. I wanted to see if she or Russell has had any dealings with this particular organization. I hope you are okay with that."

"Sure Mom. I don't mind if Collette knows. What did she say?"

"Well, she is familiar with various mission initiatives to raise funds and assist with the prevention of human trafficking but she isn't familiar with NuDawn. She will ask Russell if he has any knowledge of this group. She said she will get back to us before we leave tomorrow if she has any information."

"That would be great Mom. I guess we really need to tell Amelia too. She will not want to be the last person to know."

"I talked with her by phone this morning too but I didn't mention anything to her about this. I don't think we will see her before we go tomorrow. She said that she and Craig need some time together before he leaves town again for a few days and so they are going to stay in tonight. She works tomorrow and has the weekend off so we will get to spend some time with her then."

"That makes sense. At least by then we will have more information."

Just as Adrienne finished her last sentence, her cell rang. She got up to go back to the kitchen where she had left it on the counter and managed to get to the phone just as the caller hung up.

"It was Andre. Let me call him back."

As Adrienne made the call, I could hear her initial greeting to him and an apology for not getting to the telephone in time to answer.

"No way, that is great!" Adrienne responded. "Tell me everything. What did they say?"

As Adrienne listened, it was clear from her end of the conversation that Andre had just received and accepted the job offer with NuDawn. Despite the obvious, Adrienne was mouthing confirmation to me that he had accepted the job.

Adrienne and Andre continued talking for another few minutes. I retrieved my laptop from the bedroom and then went back out to the balcony. No time like the present to do some more research. I am glad that Andre has been able to land the position that he really wants, but I still want to make sure that Adrienne and I are prepared for tomorrow.

"Of course you can tell that he is really happy about this job offer," Adrienne said as she came back out on the balcony.

"It sounds like it! Did he get the offer that he was hoping for?"

"Yes, actually, he thought they would start him on the low end of the salary range but he said that they offered him mid-range, which is really surprising. He starts on May 6th. That is just three weeks away so he has to start looking for an apartment and getting ready to move to Miami."

"So, technically you both have offers. You just elected to think about your offer and he jumped on his."

"Yes, pretty much. Of course he is really hoping that I accept mine as well, but you know me, I have to think it through and be smart about it. It is different for him because he is out of work. I already have a great job, so the decision process is different."

"I couldn't agree more. Speaking of which, I just started to do some research. Do you want to grab your laptop and let's work on this together?"

"Sure Mom. That sounds great. What time do you want to go over to Granddad's?"

"Oh, I actually saw him this morning too. I told him we would be there mid-afternoon."

As Adrienne looked at me quizzically, I explained my earlier attempts to reach him and then my paranoia that something was wrong. I finished up with my own admonishing to myself to stop hovering.

"Mom, don't be too hard on yourself. You and Granddad have been connected at the hip taking care of Grandmother for the last twenty years. Granddad not answering his phone is weird."

"Still, I need to let him have some space and I will do my best."

Adrienne smiled and patted my arm. "You always do Mom."

Over the next two hours, Adrienne and I surfed the web. We reviewed listings of a number of non-profits and for-profits in the business of working with human trafficking. We searched for legal cases and legal challenges to the trafficking process. We reviewed legislation bills and drafts that advocate or protect the process and learned about both successes and gaps in the existing structure. The more we learned, the more intrigued we both were. The amount of facts and information were abundant and by lunch time I was wondering out loud how this huge issue was not more public.

The statistics are staggering. The annual monetary value of human trafficking is consistently reported among various sources to be in the range of $32 Billion. An estimated 1.2 million children are affected each year, yet the average age of most victims is between 18 and 24 years of age. Over 95% of the victims are physically or sexually abused while being trafficked.

As we made our list of questions and general observations about our findings in preparation for the trip tomorrow, I was overwhelmed with the prevalence and the tragedy. I was also intimately aware of Adrienne's rising passion for the topic. The details were not scaring her away, she was getting more interested. I could hear it in her voice and once again I was cognizant of her pull to this cause. As easy as it would have been to write that off on young love, I knew better. Adrienne is a practical, cautious and intelligent young woman who is doing her homework and loving the course. As I watched her finish up on our list, I knew her decision would be made soon and she would most likely be embarking on this new and strange career move that would change her in so many ways. I silently prayed for God's guidance and wisdom in this decision.

As we wrapped up our research and prepared to visit Dad, I had the realization that in the last ten days I have been exposed to two organizations helping people in times of trial and grief. First, Hospice and their valued work at the end of life and NuDawn as a warrior in the fight of human injustice.

It is amazing how life takes turns and corners. Something is tugging at me too. If I am honest with myself, a fire seems to be brewing inside of me, a prompting revealing the opportunities to make a significant difference in people's lives. I make a mental note to center my devotional time tonight on God's whispers. To understand what all of these things mean to me and to my family.

Psalms 46:10 came to mind,

"Be still and know that I am God."

I will need to *"be still"* and listen as I pray about these things. Tomorrow I will have the strength and assurance of devotion behind me as Adrienne and I embark on discovering more about this troublesome but intriguing problem and the initiatives taken to make a difference.

Before we left to go over to Dad's, I called John Stillman.

"John, I would like to help the Carter family."

"That is great Becky. When would be a good time for you?"

"I can be available tomorrow night or Saturday morning John. I will be out of town tomorrow until probably about 4:00. Otherwise, I am flexible."

"Becky, let's plan on 5:00 tomorrow afternoon. If I hear from the family that this is not a good time I will let you know."

"Thanks John. I would like for you or Anne to accompany me to meet with the family."

"One of us will be there. Anne and I will discuss it tonight and either she or I will meet you in the lobby at 5:00 tomorrow. Thank you again."

"My pleasure John, have a good evening."

"Thank you and you as well. Good-bye"

"Good-bye."

THE FRIDAY
AFTER EASTER

CHAPTER 27

Adrienne and I arrive at the designated meeting site just outside of Tampa around 9:30 am. Adrienne is reading through her notes again on our instructions. One of the staff members at the shelter, Tara Williams, will meet us at 10:00 am. She will be driving a black Ford Explorer.

As we sit and wait, I lean my head back on the headrest and close my eyes. As I silently begin to pray, Adrienne reaches over and holds my hand.

"Mom, can we pray together?"

"Of course we can. Would you like to go first?"

"Okay."

"Heavenly Father thank you for loving us. Thank you for giving me my mother, who is incredible in every way. Lord, guide us today as we learn more about children who don't have mothers who can protect them. Lord, maybe these children have been kidnapped and then sold, or maybe just sold by their own families for money to put food on the table. Lord, we don't really know or understand why these children are in this situation, but we know that you do understand this atrocity. Lord, if I am meant to help these people, in a direct way, as part of a career choice, help me to hear your command and know that I am part of your solution. I pray this in your Holy Name. Amen."

As I gently wipe a tear away, I conclude the prayer. "Father, we love you and thank you for your love and the ultimate sacrifice that you have made for us. Lord, we ask that you open our minds and hearts today to do your will. Father, guide us with your Holy Spirit and help us to understand your plans for Adrienne. Lord we ask that you place a shield of protection around these children. We ask this Lord in your blessed and Holy Name. Amen."

As I look up and give Adrienne's hand a squeeze, I notice an attractive young woman just a short distance from our vehicle. "Adrienne, I think this must be Tara."

Adrienne turned and reached to lower the car window.

"Hello, are you Tara?"

"Yes, it is nice to meet you. I didn't want to intrude on your prayer."

"Oh, thank you."

"If you will join me in my car, we can head over to the shelter."

As Adrienne and I got in to Tara's SUV, she pulled out of the parking lot and almost immediately turned down several side streets before getting on the main highway.

"We have to be careful that we are not followed," Tara said. "Although our shelter isn't advertised and its whereabouts are generally a well-kept secret, this is an ugly world, dictated by a lot of people who obviously do not value lives."

Adrienne and I exchanged looks, she in the front passenger seat and me in the backseat behind Tara.

Tara continued. "We have about a ten minute drive so I will tell you a little about the shelter on the way. We currently have 10 girls living in the shelter, ranging in age from 7 to 17 years old. 3 of the girls are from the Philippines, which is actually where a good bit of the trafficking that we see in Florida originates. We have 2 girls from Thailand, 2 from South America and 3 from the U.S.; all originating in Florida. This is a little unusual for us. We typically have more U.S. children than foreign children. The home is a three bedroom, two bath renovated home with additional living quarters for the staff onsite. We staff each home with two care-takers. Usually they are husband and wife, but occasionally we will have staff members that are not married. My husband Mark and I run this shelter. In addition, we have a part-time caseworker and other professionals on contract that deal with physical and mental care."

We turned on to a long dirt road and Tara stopped the car on a turn-off next to the road. We waited for a few minutes, Tara explaining that she again is being careful that we have not been followed. Confident that we were clear, she backed on to the dirt road and proceeded down the lane until a concrete home was visible through the trees. We parked in front of the home and behind several cars.

"The blue Acura belongs to the psychologist. She arrived while I was gone." Tara said.

We got out of the SUV and followed Tara to a door on the side of what appeared to have once been a garage, now renovated for office space.

Tara introduced us to her husband Mark and he indicated that Dr. Evans was in with Marabella; one of the residents. He also introduced us to the housekeeper, Wanda. Tara explained that because physical and sexual abuse by males is so prominent in these victims, Mark is never left in the shelter alone with the girls. There is always at least one adult female present; shelter policy. This certainly seemed reasonable.

Tara went on to explain that Mark's role is really one of safety and protection. Mark's background is in law enforcement and this is an important security feature for them at this shelter due to its remote location and distance from law enforcement offices should an issue arise.

Just as we are getting ready to tour the shelter, Dr. Evans appears and we are introduced to her as well. Adrienne and I learn that Dr. Evans has been in practice in the area for about fifteen years. She became interested in the area of human trafficking of children about five years ago and began practicing in this specialty about three years ago. Dr. Evans or another psychologist in her practice spends about ten hours a week at the shelter with the residents.

"Tara," Adrienne began, "how do you communicate with these children of different languages?"

"At first it is an issue, but most of the children have been in the U.S. for a while and have begun to pick up the language. For example, Marabella who was just seen by Dr. Evans had been in the U.S. from South America for almost two years before she was found and rescued. She was brought to America as part of a sex trade when she was twelve years old, sold by an uncle when her parents were put in jail for drug crimes. She has been at the residence now for about three months. Her English is fairly good. Other children on occasion require translation. If that is the case, we have a group of volunteers representing many languages who have been trained to work with us and the children. Mark and I are both bilingual English and Spanish, with some Mandarin. One of the case workers' that works here on a part time basis speaks French and Spanish, so we are able to communicate with most of the children."

We said our good-byes to Dr. Evans and took the brief tour of the shelter and met each of the children. Tara explained that most of the children have been in the home several months, with the exception of one of the U.S. children who had only been in the facility for three weeks. We learned later after we returned to the office to discuss the rescue, rehab and reintegration process that this fifteen year old girl had been in prostitution at the hand of her step-father since she was 9 years old. She was rescued as part of a prostitution sting, along with four other girls under the age of sixteen.

Tara and Mark spent about an hour with us, answering questions and qualifying many of the answers with variances for the type of abuse, the country of origin and the age of the girls. As I listened, my heart went out to these children. Descriptions of the nightmares and screaming, contrasted with withdrawn, fear-ridden behaviors saddened me. I admired this couple who had devoted their lives to loving these children back to safety and hopefully productive lives.

Adrienne covered her list of questions and seemed engaged in the conversation. As we wrapped up our discussion and prepared to leave, Tara indicated that Mark would drive us back to our car. Tara was needed to do an afternoon activity with the girls and Wanda was scheduled to go home. We thanked Tara for her time and headed to the Explorer with Mark.

As we drove, Mark helped us understand more about the rescue process and how children become residents at the facilities. He explained Florida is one of the largest trafficking states and that the shortage of shelters is a huge problem. When a child is rescued, they are managed by Children's Protective Services. If the situation warrants a shelter, they make every attempt to place the child if there is space availability. If there is not shelter space, then the child may be housed protectively in one of the state facilities or in temporary home placements with credentialed volunteers. The need outweighs current capacity and Mark explained how difficult this is for him and Tara, knowing that a child needs a place and the space is full.

As we neared the shopping center where we had left our SUV, I thanked Mark for his time and their willingness to share with us. Adrienne followed suit and we said our good-byes.

As we settled in the car, Adrienne looked at me and said, "Mom, I am doing this. There is nothing in the job that I do today that compares with this need, this critical need to save the children."

I nodded and put my arm around her. "Adrienne, I completely understand. I believe God has put this in front of you to use your skills and gifts to meet an important need of service to Him in caring for these children. You will do well and you will make a difference; one child at a time."

She hugged me again and we sat that way in the car for a few minutes. I was sure of one thing. In her shoes, God willing, I would have made the same choice. The need was compelling, the desire to serve a gift. I am so proud of her.

I started the car and began the drive home. Adrienne called Andre. The fact that she wanted to share with him first spoke volumes. In addition to a new career, I was pretty sure that she was also on to a new love.

I look at the time on the dashboard display. It is 2:30. My meeting with either John or Anne at the hospital is at 5:00 o'clock. Plenty of time to get back home and get my thoughts together for that meeting. What a day!

As I drove and Adrienne talked with Andre, I remembered that I had turned my cell phone off as a courtesy during our visit at the shelter. I reached for my phone and noticed five voice mail messages. At the next traffic signal I dialed voice mail and put the Bluetooth in my ear, so as not to interrupt Adrienne's conversation.

Two messages were from Amelia wanting to know our plans and whether we could meet her for dinner around 7:00. One message was from Dad, one from John Stillman confirming that he would be attending the meeting with me and one from Mary at the office.

I returned Mary's call first. Amelia would be next. I would catch up with Dad when I arrived home. Mary assured me that everything at the office was going well. She discussed with me one time-sensitive filing on the Sampson case and we discussed next steps on the document and process. I offered to come in to the office to review the filing but she indicated Doug Andrews was in the office and had offered to take care of it this afternoon. I thanked Mary and told her that I would see her Monday morning.

Adrienne was still talking to Andre so I dialed Amelia.

"Hi Mom! What are you two doing with your day off?"

This reminded me that we had not discussed Adrienne's opportunity or our visit today with Amelia. "The two of us have had a fairly exciting day. We will have to catch you up on it later at dinner. What time will you get off?"

"I should be off at 7:00. I could meet you around 7:30. Or if the two of you wouldn't mind, an extra half-hour could allow for a much needed shower and change."

"Eight o'clock is fine with us Amelia. Do you want to meet at Captain Harry's or do you want to go somewhere else?"

"Captain Harry's is good. I will call ahead and see if I can get us a table on the water."

"That sounds good honey. We will see you then."

"Okay Mom. I can't wait to hear about your exciting day. You kind of have my interest peaked."

"We will clue you in when we see you tonight."

"Okay, see you then. Love you, bye.

"Love you too, bye."

As I hung up the phone Adrienne was just finishing her call as well. "Andre is heading down to Miami tonight. He is planning to drive straight through so that he can begin looking for a place to live Monday. I did ask him if he could stop by here on the way but he said that they need to head directly to Miami because Todd, his friend that is helping him move, has to be back to work on Monday."

"Well, that makes sense. I am glad he has someone to help him with the drive and the move."

"Yes, Todd seems to be a good guy. I have only met him once."

"Switching gears, Amelia is going to meet us at Captain Harry's at 8:00. I have the meeting at the hospital this afternoon with hospice. Would you like to go spend some time with Granddad or would you like to stay at the condo and I will come back and get you later?"

"I think I want to stay at the condo Mom. I need to call NuDawn and accept their offer and then I really want some time to think through all these changes and what I need to get done."

"Ok, that sounds like a plan. Let's go home now and you can get your things done and I can regroup for my visit this afternoon."

We drove the final few miles in silence, each thinking our own thoughts. Adrienne had clearly made her decision and now she was in her organization and action mode. She would be unstoppable until everything was in place. As we parked and headed in to the condo, I realized that the forward momentum of my children; Amelia's wedding and Adrienne's new opportunities, have occupied my thoughts and left very little time for me to be with my own thoughts and process the grief I feel with the loss of my mother. Maybe this is a good thing. Looking forward, living life and sharing hope for the future. The grief is still there, but the hope of tomorrow is a blessing worth looking toward.

CHAPTER 28

J ohn Stillman is already in the hospital lobby when I arrive.

"Hello John."

"Hello Becky. It is good to see you again. Thank you for agreeing to meet with the Carters."

"You are welcome."

"I spoke with Deidre earlier today and she has gathered a few of the family members together. Rather than meet in the hospital room, I have secured a conference room from the hospital for the meeting. We may end up in the hospital room with Mrs. Carter later but I thought it would be better to at least initially meet away from the room."

"That sounds good John. Since I have not done this before, are there any special thoughts or pearls of wisdom that you would like to share? Any topics that I should stay away from?"

"Not really. Our goal here today is to listen and respond. We don't really know what Deidre saw in your family that was of comfort to her. Let's listen and draw on our knowledge and experiences."

"Okay."

When we arrive in the conference room, four of the family members are present. As we are introduced to each of them, it is clear that they are all hesitant about this meeting. As I think about it I am surprised that this has not come to mind for me before now. While I was worrying about my hesitancy, it didn't occur to me that they may not want to participate.

John began the visit by introducing himself and then me. As he describes the role of hospice, I glance around the room. Deidre is in her early to mid-forties. She is an attractive woman but looks as if the stress and strain is taking a toll on her. Her attractive features are dulled by the dark circles under her eyes and the general fatigue in her demeanor. Her father, George, is sitting next to her with his hands on the table looking intently at John. He looks tired as well and his eyes mist with emotion as John talks about the natural process of death as part of the life cycle. Next to George is Danny; Deidre's brother. Danny looks to be slightly younger than Deidre and is holding his hands tightly in his lap. He frequently looks down at his hands and seems to want to be anyplace but here. Lastly, Deidre's brother Brock is at the end of the table. He is by far the youngest of the children represented here and seems to be listening intently to John. From years of experience in the courtroom, and sizing up people quickly, I imagine that Brock is the most open of the family members to Deidre's invitation to meet with us.

As John finishes his introduction to Hospice, he looks over at me and asks if I would like to add anything to his comments. I look at the family and then at Deidre. "Deidre thank you for requesting to meet with me. I know a little bit about the difficulty that your family is currently facing and I am happy to share my experiences, but before I do, I would like to ask how you all are doing." As I added this last statement, I made eye contact with each of the family members.

For a few moments, no one spoke. Finally Deidre addressed me and her family together. "Mrs. Kennedy, we are struggling. All of us are trying to cope with Mom being in the condition that she is in and knowing that she will not get better, only worse. We are a family that has always revolved around Mom and although she has been going downhill and we have had to pull back on some of our reliance on her, we can't seem to talk or communicate as a family. Last week when I sat in the lobby and watched your family just before they said good-bye to their mother, grandmother or friend, it was as if they were on the edge of something bright instead of a tragedy. I don't know if that makes sense."

Before I could say anything, Danny spoke up. "Deidre, Mom is dying. We have been on this horse in this rodeo for a while. It has been at least seven or eight years where we haven't been depending on Mom for the basics. I don't know what you want this nice lady here to say that is going to make everything better, but maybe she can. I don't know."

I wait a moment to see if anyone else wants to speak. After a few moments George started, clearly emotional. "My wife, Evelyn, has been the heart and the glue for our family. Ever since she has started to lose her memory, we all have been trying to work it out but somehow it just ain't working."

Deidre looked at me and said, "I think it has to do with faith and believing in a hereafter. Do you think that Mrs. Kennedy?"

"Please call me Becky," I said as I smiled at Deidre and then the others around the room. "Deidre, I can't begin to tell you or your family how to grieve and how to fill the void that is left by your mother in what was clearly such an influential role in your family. What I can tell you is some of the things I have learned and the conclusions that I have come to as part of my own journey."

"My mother was sick for twenty-two years. She was an amazing woman, so full of life and so vibrant." I looked at George. "Clearly, she was the love of my father's life. I have learned a few things that may be helpful for you. The first is, you have to have patience. This disease and the process of decline can wear on you until you feel like you don't have one more ounce of tolerance and you think you are going to snap. I have learned to bolster my patience over the years by remembering back to a time when my mother was at her best. I often think that if she was her old self, she would hate the position her disease placed the family in and would hurt knowing that we had to go through the pain that every caregiver feels as this disease process takes over." As I spoke, I could see all of the family watching me closely; waiting probably for some pearl of wisdom that I wasn't sure I could deliver for them.

"The second thing that I know is that I could not do this without my faith in God. I don't know what your personal beliefs are, but I know that my comfort and peace in dealing with both my mother and my husband's death rest in knowing that both of them are joyful in their place in God's Kingdom."

"That is what we are missing," replied Deidre. "That is what I saw in your family when they were in the waiting room. I didn't know that you had also lost your husband. I am sorry."

"Thank you. Yes, Roger was killed in a car accident two years ago."

"Mrs. Kennedy, I am sorry for both of your losses and I do mean and intend respect, but I am not buying the God thing," Danny said. "When my mom dies, she is gone, ashes to ashes and dust to dust."

"I wish I believed in what you say Becky," George said. "I wish that this was just a turn in the road and that I could spend forever with Evelyn. It just doesn't make sense to me."

"George, God is bigger than our rational capabilities. If you think about God in the limits and confines of our minds, you are absolutely right. We can't imagine God's love and His power when we think about those things within the realm of our capacity. But God's capacity is so much greater and I will personally attest to His presence in my life, my love and my decisions every step of the way. If you would like to talk with someone further about this, I would recommend my pastor, Russell James."

"I would like to talk to him," Deidre said. "Would he be willing to talk to us?"

"Of course he would. I will give him a call when I leave here."

There was silence for a few moments and then I asked, "Is there anything going on with Evelyn's condition and the family decisions that I can help with?"

"One of the things that we are trying to deal with is how much does Mom hear and know? Dad wants us here all the time but Mom doesn't know we are here and it is a problem with trying to be at work and here," Brock said.

All eyes looked at me and I looked at each of them. "Brock you raise a good point and I think it is something that each of you have to decide within your own personal situations. None of us really know what an Alzheimer patient knows or takes in toward the end of life unless they are able to communicate. My mother didn't speak at all during her last seven years. Does Evelyn seem to know what goes on around her?"

"No. Mom speaks gibberish and when we could understand her several months ago, she thought we were people from her childhood, not her children," Danny said.

"I know that is hard Danny, I have been there myself. But again what we don't know is how much she is really aware of her surroundings. On the other hand, I know that my father needed me by his side. This is difficult for your Dad and George I bet that having your children with you makes this more bearable. Is that right?"

George had begun to weep some and I knew it was how he felt. I doubted however, given the brief time that I had with the family that anyone here ever communicated that way.

George nodded and Deidre put her arm around him.

"This is a time for family. Each of you in your own way is dealing with this loss. You need each other. When someone I know has asked how I am managing as a caretaker/daughter in my mother's long illness, I always reply, "I am just loving her through it." At the end of the day, really, that is all we can do."

Deidre had started to cry as well and I reached my hand across the table to hers. I looked at George and then Danny and Brock and finally to John. John put his hand on my shoulder as a show of support and asked the family if they had anything else that they wanted to discuss.

"I would like to ask you to pray with us if you wouldn't mind. When your family was in the waiting room they all held hands and prayed and I felt such comfort," Deidre said.

"Deidre, I would be happy to pray with you." I looked around the room and saw some discomfort on Danny's face but Brock and George didn't seem uneasy with the request.

"Danny, is it okay with you if we say a prayer?" I asked.

"Sure."

"Then let's bow our heads and pray."

"Dear Heavenly Father, thank you for this time today to talk with George, Deidre, Danny and Brock. Lord you know that their hearts are heavy with Evelyn's illness and the decline in her condition. Lord, we ask you to be with Evelyn. Surround her with Your comfort and peace Lord. Let her feel Your arms around her with each passing moment. Lord, we ask you to be with the Carter family in this trying time. Lord lift their hearts and open their eyes to your love and grace. Surround them with the warmth of your Spirit and help them to come to know the gift of eternal life that you bore on the cross. We ask these things of you Father in Your Holy Name. Amen."

As I completed the prayer and looked up, George and Deidre were crying and Brock had tears in his eyes. Danny hung his head and wiped his eyes. I stood up and everyone else followed. I reached out to give Deidre and George a hug. As I did, Deidre said, "How do I give my life to Christ? I want to do that."

"Deidre, you just have to invite him in to your heart. Do you want to do that now?"

"Yes, I do. Can you help me?"

"Yes, Deidre I would be honored."

I put my hand on her shoulder and John Stillman reached in and put one hand on my shoulder and one on Deidre's.

"Deidre, do you believe that Jesus Christ is the Son of God?"

"I do".

"Are you willing to commit the Holy Spirit of God into your heart and live for Him and glorify His Kingdom?"

"Yes."

"Then Deidre, by asking God in to your life, you are considered to be born anew. I would like to have you meet Pastor James and complete your profession of faith with baptism and begin to learn about serving God as a believer."

"Okay," Deidre said through tears. As she hugged me again, she was beaming. George was crying and hugging her and Brock had his arm around her. Danny quietly left the room and headed back down the hall.

"I would like to meet your mother," I said to Deidre.

"That would be great Becky. Come with us".

As we left the conference room and walked down the hall toward Evelyn's room, the events of the last hour replayed in my head. Who knew God had such awesome plans for this meeting? A new Christian—how great was that?

As John and I followed Deidre, George and Brock in to room 331, I prepared myself. With the death of my mother just days ago, in this very hospital, I wasn't sure how I would react but I knew it was an important conclusion to this family's healing and our time today.

Danny was already in the room, sitting by his mother's side, holding her hand. Evelyn was frail and looked very small under her hospital sheet and blanket. Her eyes were open, but confused and distant. She smiled when George said her name and I walked to the bedside.

"Hi Evelyn, my name is Becky. I just had the chance to meet your family. I know you are proud of them and they were just telling me what a wonderful wife and mother that you have been." I smile as I look at her. She returns the smile and I think back to how long ago it has been since I saw my mother smile in response to me. Three years, four years, I'm not sure? What a gift for this family that their mother can see the end of her days still smiling, even if she is confused about why she is smiling.

I stood back from the bed, shook George's hand, then Brocks. Danny nodded but did not offer his hand to me. I hugged Deidre again and told her I would speak with Pastor James shortly and I was sure he would be in touch with her.

John and I left the room and walked down the corridor toward the elevators. Once outside, John thanked me. "Becky, thank you for meeting with the Carters; that was an incredible meeting."

"John, I did the only thing I could do, I spoke the truth. In doing that, God took over that meeting. Deidre accepting God on the spot was a beautiful thing. I hope that the others follow her lead. This family needs to know and trust that this is the end of one life but another one, a better one follows our time here on earth."

As I looked in to John's eyes I saw love and admiration there. Shocked and surprised, I stood facing him unable to look away for a moment.

"Becky, you are incredible. Please let me buy you a glass of wine or a cup of coffee."

"I am sorry John. I am meeting my girls this evening for dinner. Adrienne heads back to Charlotte on Sunday and Amelia and I are spending every possible moment with her. Maybe we can do that another time?"

"I would love that. Thanks again."

"Thank you John for being here. I will see you again soon."

As I walked away, I felt almost giddy. I had been part of a life changed today. How awesome was that! And surprisingly I feel an unexpected attraction to John Stillman. He is handsome, but that really isn't it. It is his presence, his strength, his demeanor that is attractive in a way that I haven't felt or noticed since Roger.

Thank goodness I am meeting the girls and have a good reason to decline more time with John. I need to think through this attraction and my feelings. A glass of wine, feeling the way I do right now, could be a recipe for a relationship. Although normally I would have shunned the idea immediately, there is just something special about John.

As I got in the car and pulled out of the parking lot, I called Pastor James. I wanted to make sure that he was in touch with Deidre and her family as soon as possible.

CHAPTER 29

A drienne and I arrived at Captain Harry's before Amelia. We had called Dad to invite him for dinner but he had said 8:00 was too late to eat and that the girls and I should enjoy some time together. We promised we would see him tomorrow for lunch and he was happy with that plan. Tomorrow we would have to tell him about Adrienne's new career.

While I had been meeting with the Carter's, Adrienne had spoken with both the hiring manager for her position at NuDawn, as well as the human resource officer. She accepted the position and confirmed her salary and benefits, her start date which would be June 15, two weeks after Amelia's wedding, and had learned that they would pay for one month in a transitional apartment while she looked for a place to live. Although her start date is seven weeks away, the June 15th date worked best for them and it worked for being available the week before the wedding to share in all of the planning and excitement.

"I am still thinking about how much notice to give my work. In some cases they dismiss you as soon as you give notice since they do not want certain positions to have access to new product development information. We are so short staffed in the legal department that I don't think they will make that decision. I could continue to work on the projects that I am already aware of and just not be exposed to new development or new client information."

"How much vacation do you have left?"

"I have eight days. I had planned to use five of them for Amelia's wedding but I won't have to do that now."

"Why don't you give your employer a four week notice and come down here two weeks before Amelia's wedding and hang with us? You could work on a tan; get a healthy glow for that beautiful dress."

"I could do that."

"Do what?" Amelia asked as she came around the table and sat down.

Adrienne and I both looked at each other and then at Amelia.

"What is going on?" Amelia asked. "Both of you look like you are harboring national secrets."

Adrienne looked at Amelia and said, "Perhaps you should order a glass of wine first, you are going to need it."

"Uh-oh, what on earth have you two been up to?"

I got the waitress's attention and Amelia ordered a glass of Chablis.

"Okay, spill it. What is going on?"

Adrienne started from the beginning and shared the history of the NuDawn opportunity from beginning to end. She included bits and pieces about Andre but I noticed that she steered away from too much information. My guess was she didn't want Amelia, or anyone else for that matter, making an assumption that the decision was about a hopeful relationship.

"So, you are resigning from your posh job and moving to Florida to save women and children who are traded basically as slaves and sex addicts?"

"Well, in a nutshell I guess that is it," Adrienne replied.

"Good for you!" Amelia jumped up and hugged her sister. "You will be closer to us, just a couple of hours away, and you will be doing something that you are passionate about! That deserves a celebration." Amelia picked up her wine glass and Adrienne and I followed her lead in a toast for much success and happiness.

"Now," Amelia said, "I am a little ticked at not having advanced knowledge. What is up with that Adrienne?"

"I am sorry. I didn't tell Mom either until Wednesday. I wanted to tell you both in person and then when Grandmother got so sick, and the funeral, I just didn't think it was the right time. I wasn't trying to exclude either of you."

"Alright, you are forgiven. Now, before you start thinking about keeping any more secrets, tell me about Andre. And don't think I didn't see your eyes glitter and your cheeks flush when you talked about him."

Adrienne's cheeks turned an even darker shade of red at her sister's blunt acknowledgement of what was more obvious than Adrienne had intended.

"Amelia! I can't believe you said that."

"Adrienne, as soon as you mentioned his name, you were all dreamy-eyed and nervous. Now, tell me about him and I am going to assume that Mother has already heard about him so that makes two secrets that you have kept from me."

As Adrienne tells Amelia about Andre, I watch both of my girls together. They are smart, kind, beautiful and as different as night and day. I want to cherish this moment, here on the deck, overlooking the water, sharing this wonderful time in my daughter's lives. I suddenly wonder if Mother is watching, if she has a place where she can look down on her girls, all three of us, and share this moment. She would be proud and she would love the girl-talk. Mother always said that she was happiest when she was with Laura and me when we were growing up. She could have been involved in many more social and charity events but she always said her time at home in the evenings was time well spent when she could spend it with us. I understand what she meant. These moments are so rare and so precious. And as these two girls begin to build their own families that will likely become even more rare.

Amelia's cell phone rang and she hit the ignore button, something unusual for her.

"Who was that?" I asked.

"Craig. I am a little annoyed with him so I will make him wait. I will call him back later. He knows we are having dinner together."

"What did he do?" asked Adrienne.

"It is what he is not doing that is upsetting me. He is supposed to fly these two trips, leaving this morning and returning on Sunday night. Now he has volunteered to run two more legs, just because he wants to rub elbows with this rich and famous musician. So now he will be home on Wednesday night and then leaves out again Friday for another four day assignment. We have so much to do before the wedding but we are never around at the same time to get things done."

"Maybe the extra money is the motivator. This wedding and honeymoon is expensive," Adrienne suggested.

"That is not it. It is his ego. He likes to puff up and talk about all of the celebrities that he flies around. Don't get me wrong, I get excited too sometimes with the celebrities that he shuttles around, but this time I am upset. We have plans and they are playing second fiddle to a fiddle player!"

We all laughed at her play on words and eventually she was laughing too. I understand her frustration with Craig, and frankly his ego is usually the only issue that I have with him, but the reality is that this mobile career as a pilot is his choice and that has been the case all along. They will have to strike a balance and a set of game rules to avoid future issues.

Our dinner came and the food was delicious. As the dessert menu was delivered by our waitress we all three took a look but decided to avoid the calories. After our dress fitting earlier this week, we knew that we had better watch our waistlines for the next few weeks.

The Friday night band began to play in the corner and we sat back to enjoy the music for a while. Amelia saw a couple of her girlfriends and stopped over to sit with them for a few minutes. Adrienne had a smile on her face and we both were enjoying the crisp breeze off of the water.

"Mom, I am glad that I am going to be living closer to you and Amelia and of course Granddad. I forgot how nice it is to be here."

"Adrienne, I am excited about that too. It will be great to get to see you more often and of course I will want to know all about your new job. Maybe I can come down and help you decorate your new place. Amelia would probably like to do that too."

"Yes, well I guess my lease expiring isn't an issue any more. I will have a new lease in another state. I feel really good about this move Mom."

"I do too Adrienne."

Amelia came back to the table and said it was time for her to call it a night. We gathered our things and walked together. Amelia had managed to park next to us and so we leaned on the cars for a few minutes and made plans for tomorrow.

Since Craig would be away, Amelia was open to spending the day with us. We agreed to meet at Dad's around 11:00, see how he is doing and decide on the rest of the day then.

Sunday Adrienne's flight leaves at 3:00 pm. Both girls want to go to church and then we can all take Adrienne to the airport.

Adrienne and I both gave Amelia a hug and headed home. Tomorrow is something to look forward to and Sunday will come too soon.

THE SATURDAY
AFTER EASTER

Chapter 30

W hen Adrienne and I arrived at Dad's on Saturday morning, Amelia was already there.

"Hi Dad."

"Hi Sweetheart, how are you doing?"

"We are doing great. What are you two up to?

"Amelia and I are just having another cup of coffee and we just got off of the telephone with Laura."

"Oh good; what is she doing today?"

"She was just checking on us, said she misses us already."

"I am sure she does. I miss her too."

"Pour a cup of coffee and let's go sit out on the dock. It is a nice morning and Amelia and I already have the chairs set up out there."

"Sounds good Dad."

Adrienne and I poured our coffee and noticed that Dad had flavored creamer in the refrigerator left over from some thoughtful person's delivery following the funeral. She and I both added the caramel flavor to our coffee and went outside to sit on the dock.

The day is beautiful. Sailboats are out on the bay and the ripple on the water looks like dancing crystals in the sunlight. As we sit down, I take a good look at Dad. The stress and emotion is on the surface of his expression and it seems that in moments he may be in tears. I am concerned about his sadness but know him well enough to know that he does not want to be emotional in front of Amelia and Adrienne. He and I will have plenty of time for that later. Dad needs something to distract him for the moment, and I know just the thing.

"Dad, Adrienne has some pretty big news. Adrienne, why don't you tell your Granddad about your new job?"

Dad looked from me to Adrienne and I could see the relief on his face. Then the curiosity took over as he considered "big news".

"Well Granddad, I am going to be moving back to Florida!"

"What? That is great news. Are you coming back here?"

That Adrienne is one smart cookie. Leading with the relocation back to Florida as the beginning of the story is one way to defuse concerns that I am sure Dad will have about the nature of the work.

"No," Adrienne replied. "Actually I am moving to Miami. But the good news is that I will only be a few hours in a car from you instead of a couple of hours by airplane."

"Miami! What in the world are you going to be doing in Miami?"

As Adrienne began explaining Children's NuDawn to Dad, I watched him as he listened. Adrienne was keeping the description pretty high level, leaving out some of the details around potential danger that she may be exposed to on occasion as part of her role in the company. Dad however didn't miss a beat.

"Adrienne, this is honorable work but you are going to be experiencing a really dark side of culture. Is there any risk to you or are you primarily behind a desk?"

Leave it to Dad to zoom in on the heart of the matter.

"Granddad, most of the time I will be dealing with the legal matters; paper, phone calls, contracts, etc. But, I can't lie to you. There will be times when I will be traveling internationally to facilitate safe recovery of children. The really dangerous stuff is done by people who are trained in protective enforcement, but some risk is inherent in the work itself."

Dad and Amelia are looking at Adrienne intently.

"Adrienne, you be careful," Dad said. Then he turned to me and asked, "Are you okay with this Becky?"

"Yes Dad, actually I am very good with it. Adrienne and I have had a chance to do our research, visit one of the shelters nearby and pray together. I believe that this opportunity has been put in front of her as a way for her to serve God through serving these children. She is passionate about this and she will be fine."

Adrienne smiles at me. Having her back with questions from her Grandfather is always appreciated by both of my girls. His interrogation tactics can at times be difficult, although today he is engaged and accepting.

"Adrienne, you are a good person and have turned in to a nice young lady. You give this the best you have and always turn your questions and worries over to God. I wish you the best with these children."

"Thanks Granddad."

"And, I will be glad to see you more often!"

As Adrienne smiled at Dad, he told her he loved her and she replied in kind. The news had transformed his face from raw emotion, no doubt with Mother on his mind, to genuine love exchanged; a beautiful sight.

"So Granddad, what do you want to do today?" Amelia asked.

"Well, I was out at the gravesite yesterday and they have your Grandmother's headstone up. I would like it if we could all go out to the cemetery together."

"Dad, we would like that. Do you want to stop and get some flowers on the way?"

"No, I took some pink roses yesterday and I called the florist to have a vase of artificial pink roses made so that she will always have flowers. I will put real ones out every now and then but I think the artificial is the best on an everyday basis."

"That is thoughtful Granddad," Amelia said.

As we finished visiting on the dock, Dad asked Amelia how the planning was going on the wedding. She seemed to have worked through her frustration with Craig from last night, because she was clearly gushing over him this morning.

"Granddad, last time we talked you hadn't decided whether you are going to wear your personal tuxedo or rent one. If you are going to rent one, we need to get you an appointment."

"Amelia, let's rent one. I am walking you down the aisle and I want to look my best. The one that I have is older and this is too important."

"Okay Granddad. I will get an appointment set up for some time next week if that will work for you."

"That will be fine honey. I don't have much on my schedule these days."

We decided to head over to the cemetery and I coaxed Dad in to letting me drive. The four of us rode over together and found Mother's gravesite easily. As Dad had said, a dozen pink roses with baby's breath and ferns sat in the bronze vase on her headstone.

The headstone read:

Gloria Denise Bridges
Loving Wife and Mother

Her Soul is Safe with God
Listen as she sings with Angels

01/14/1930-03/30/2013

"Dad, it is beautiful," I said as I put my arm around him.

"It is nice. I think she would have liked it."

Both girls hugged their grandfather and we all had tears in our eyes. It is so difficult to say good-bye. I know that having Adrienne home and being busy with her has saved me these last few days but I also know that beginning Monday when things are back to normal, the void will be evident and the grief possibly overwhelming. I can't imagine how Dad must feel. He has spent the last sixty years with her and now she is gone.

I left the girls to go back to the car and get tissues. Dad, Amelia and Adrienne positioned themselves on one of the benches near Mom's gravesite. They were holding hands and talking quietly when I returned.

"Granddad, how did you know that she was the one?" Adrienne asked.

"Your Grandmother was beautiful, as beautiful as the two of you, although she had more of your features Adrienne. Of course it wasn't just her beauty that I fell in love with, but it is what I noticed first. She was playing the piano at a hymn-fest at the church that I was attending while I was stationed in North Carolina before I went overseas in the war. I saw her playing and she just captivated me. Afterwards, there was a cake and coffee reception and I got my nerve up to go over and speak to her. When she smiled, I thought I was drowning. I couldn't breathe, she was so beautiful. After that I was in church every time the doors were open," he laughed. "Finally, one day I asked her if she wanted to go to a play in town. It wasn't really proper to go out at night together on a first date, so we went to the afternoon matinee. During the play, I held her hand and I knew she was the one. Of course, we didn't get married until after the war, but she waited for me to come home. Knowing that she was waiting for me and praying for me kept me strong during the hard days in Europe during WWII. She told me later that it was love at first sight for her too. She said that I was strong and distinguished and so mannerly. I think both of us just knew and we have kept the fires burning every day since. I will miss her but I know that she is in heaven waiting on me. We have been separated by circumstances before, we will endure this separation as well."

"Granddad, that is a great story," Adrienne said.

"It has been a great life Adrienne. I have no regrets. I wish both of your girls the happiness that your Grandmother and I had. I only wish your Dad could have been with us now."

At the mention of Roger, tears surfaced and began spilling over before I could control them. I grabbed one of the tissues and wiped my eyes. Amelia and Adrienne both started crying as well and for a few minutes we shared the raw grief that comes from losing a husband and father unexpectedly.

"I am sorry girls. I didn't mean to upset you," Dad said.

"Dad, it is okay. We are just a little emotional now with losing Mom and remembering Roger. We know that he greeted Mom in heaven with arms wide open."

The girls both smiled and wiped their eyes. Dad stood and we followed him back to the car. As we walked, I stopped and looked back at Mother's grave. I would come again, alone, so that I could have some quiet time here. I turned and joined Dad and the girls in the car. We were all wiping our eyes as we pulled away.

"Where to now?" I asked.

"Let's take a ride Mom," Adrienne said. "Maybe we can find a café or restaurant that we haven't tried and have lunch."

It was doubtful that anyone really cared about food right now, but I sensed that Adrienne wanted the togetherness. I thought about her leaving tomorrow and how hard that would be for her and for me.

"That sounds like a great idea," I said. "Dad, are you up for that?"

"Yes, I think that sounds good. There is a new restaurant down by the Adam's old place on River Drive. I don't know the name of it but some of the men at church were talking about it a few weeks ago. Of course, taking care of your Mother, I didn't really care about taking the time to check it out. Maybe today is the day."

THE SUNDAY
AFTER EASTER

CHAPTER 31

S unday was cloudy when I woke up and a drizzle of rain
combined with the clouds gave a dank, gray gloom to the
view of the ocean from the balcony. I decided to drink my
coffee inside and had just sat down on the barstool with the Sunday
paper when Adrienne came out of her room. Dressed in her PJ pants
with assorted crazy high heel designs all over them and a matching
tank, she looked like my daughter memories of her growing up. It
was easy to remember those days and more difficult to transition
those memories to the confident young woman that I am proud of
today.

"Good morning Mom."

"Good morning sweetheart. Did you sleep okay?"

"I did. I slept great."

"I have some yogurt and granola or I can fix you some eggs.
What sounds good?"

"Coffee first, then probably yogurt," Adrienne said as she poured
herself a large mug of coffee.

I handed Adrienne a section of the paper and we both read in
silence for a few minutes. I excused myself to go get a shower for
church and Adrienne said she would get dressed too.

When we arrived at church, Russell and Collette were both in
the foyer of the church. Collette hugged the girls and then pulled
Adrienne and me aside to hear about the trip on Friday. Russell joined
us and Adrienne and I shared some of the highlights of the trip and

then Adrienne's decision to take the job. Russell and Collette both gave her a hug and Russell asked if she minded if the church prayed for her today. Adrienne said that she didn't mind, just as Dad came in the door. Russell left to prepare for the service and Collette gave Dad a big hug and asked if she could sit with us today.

"Of course you can," Dad said. "You can sit with me every Sunday if you want. Russell is in the pulpit and Becky and Amelia are in the choir. We might as well sit together!"

"I may take you up on that Dan, you better watch out," Collette teased.

Amelia came in then and we all proceeded down the aisle to get seated. Since Amelia and I had not been available for choir practice this week, we would sit in the congregation instead of in the choir loft. Dad would enjoy us all together anyway, so that was a good thing.

The choir sang their prelude and then Russell offered a prayer. Following the prayer, Russell announced that he wanted to change up the service a little. Our church is small enough and we all know each other well enough to manage changes on the fly, so this departure is not totally new to the congregation.

"I have a favor to ask of the congregation. Adrienne, could you come up here with me?"

Adrienne, somewhat surprised, got up and walked to the front of the church.

Russell put his arm around her and addressed the congregation. "Adrienne has given me permission to have the congregation pray for her today. She hasn't yet given her notice to her employer so this is all on the QT until she is able to do that."

The congregation smiled at that, knowing that Adrienne works in Charlotte and the chance of giving up the secret was unlikely by anyone here.

"Adrienne is getting ready to do something very special and she will need our diligence in prayer for her impact on God's Kingdom and her safety. Beginning in June, Adrienne is going to work for an organization that's mission is to intercede on the sex and slave trade of children. This organization finds children who are in this horrible circumstance and transitions them in to safe environments. As we know, Jesus said to love the little children and the old familiar song adds, "...all the children of the world." Well, that is the passion Adrienne has found in this work and I want to offer up a prayer today, in front of this congregation, and I want us to be vigilant as a congregation in praying for the success of this organization to change the face of this problem."

The room is silent, you could hear a pin drop. Adrienne is looking and listening to Pastor James. I know standing in front of a congregation, center of attention, is not something Adrienne is comfortable with, yet I know that she is touched by Pastor James' heart and his desire for the congregation to pray for her.

"Let us pray."

As we bow our heads, I see Russell reach for her hand, still with his arm around her shoulders.

"Father God, thank you for Adrienne Kennedy. Thank you for her heart. Thank you for her love and service to you and thank you for loving her and giving her the spirit to serve. God, you love the children of the world and we know it breaks your heart Lord when children are mistreated and abused. Lord we ask you to honor this work that Adrienne is getting ready to do. Fill her with the strength, knowledge and fortitude to use her gifts to your glory and in a way that changes the children's lives. Lord, keep her safe and keep her focus on those things that please you and provide for Your Kingdom. Lord, as a church remind us to be vigilant in our prayers. Lord, we thank you and we pray this in Your Holy Name. Amen."

As Pastor James finished the prayer, several of the congregation gathered at the front of the church to hug Adrienne and to let her know that they would be praying for her. I wiped the tears from my eyes and got out of my seat to join them and her. I stood by Adrienne's side as she was greeted by each of those fellow church members who wished her well. Many offered condolences to both of us on Mom's passing. After the last person had shared a moment with Adrienne, we went back to our seats for the rest of the service.

"Mom, that was so unexpected but so nice," Adrienne whispered as the service continued. "Pastor James is amazing."

I smiled at her and gave her hand a squeeze. It was a wonderful thing for Russell to do and I was grateful for this church community.

After church was over, we dropped Dad and Amelia's cars at his house and we all rode in my SUV together to the airport. After parking, we made our way in to the terminal to get Adrienne checked in. The only airport restaurant was on the visitor side of check-in and so we found a table and ordered lunch. Adrienne's flight didn't leave for another hour and a half so we had plenty of time to spend some last moments with her.

"So Adrienne, have you decided when you are going to give notice at your job and how much time you are planning to give?" I asked.

"I am going to give notice tomorrow. I think it is only fair to be forthright about it and besides, I want to get the notification behind me and begin to prepare for the move and everything. I figure if I give four weeks' notice, my last day of work will be on May 11th. Amelia's wedding is June 2nd, so I will have a couple of weeks to get things packed up and finished in Charlotte and then a week or ten days before the wedding to be here with you guys. I start work there on June 15th."

"That sounds good to me. I would like to plan on helping you with your move. Once you have talked with your employer and you know your move date, I will fly up and help you with the packing and then drive back with you."

"Thanks Mom that would be great."

As we finished our lunch, Adrienne noticed that the security lines were getting longer. She hugged each of us and gathered her carry-on bag and purse and headed to the security area. We all watched her and gave a last wave before she went through the check point.

"I miss her already," Amelia said.

"It will be nice to have her back near home," Dad said.

"Yes it will. I am excited for her. She has found a passion and she will be close by. It is all good. Now, we have a move and a wedding! No one can say that we are boring."

"No kidding Mom," Amelia confirmed.

We gathered our things and headed back out to the airport parking garage. The next few weeks were going to be a whirlwind; probably just what all of us needed. *"Thank you God"*, I silently whispered.

THE WEDDING

June 2nd dawns bright and beautiful. The weather report is forecasting rain this afternoon but I have my hopes up that the 'scattered showers' will scatter somewhere else.

Amelia is simply stunning in her dress. Getting dressed with the wedding party has been fun, lots of laughs and nervous anticipation. This is the moment, all of the planning completed, a day to enjoy this wedding celebration.

As I wait my turn to walk down the aisle on Robert's arm, I couldn't be happier for Amelia. She and Craig both seem truly content and excited about their future together. Of course, I have shed a few tears in private this morning, wishing that Roger could be here to walk her down the aisle and Mother could see her beautiful granddaughter marry today. But I know they are here with us in spirit, joyously sharing in the celebration.

One last glance over my shoulder at the wedding party and then on cue I walk down the aisle on Robert's arm. He is handsome in his tuxedo and although he is not an official member of Craig's groomsmen, he agreed to Amelia's request to escort me down the aisle.

Once seated, I look around and smile at our family in the front rows. Laura and Bob are seated on my row to my left. Next to them are Caitlin and the children; Alex and Brooke. Behind me are Alicia and her husband Kevin, with their children Cody and Elise. Laura surprised them with tickets to Florida so that they could attend the wedding. Thankfully, Kevin had been able to get the time off and it is wonderful to have them here. Chris is sitting next to Elise and clearly enjoying her one year old antics.

Adrienne did decide to invite Andre and he is sitting next to Chris. They have connected and I am glad to see the comradery. I had the chance to meet Andre on a visit to Miami with Adrienne and I am already impressed with him. He is truly a nice young man and clearly smitten with Adrienne.

The opening notes to Mendelssohn signal that the procession is beginning and I turn to watch as each of the bridesmaids join the groomsmen and Pastor James at the front of the church. As Adrienne walks, just ahead of her sister, I catch her smile after she makes eye contact with Andre. Yes, this is definitely a romance taking shape and I am pleased with her choice. As she nears my church pew her gaze finds mine and she smiles again. Her beauty is undeniable and her periwinkle blue dress and pastel pink pearls compliment her so well.

As the notes grow louder and more pronounced we all stand as Amelia rounds the corner from the back of the church on her grandfather's arm. She is stunning and Dad looks so handsome and happy. Unavoidable, tears well up in my eyes and I reach for my hidden handkerchief to dab at them before they spill over the lashes and down my face.

Amelia approaches my row and reaches out her hand to me. I notice that she is wearing mother's sapphire ring. Holding my hand, she kisses me on each cheek. After, she removes a white rose from her bouquet and hands it to me. Although I know that she has planned this, and we practiced in rehearsal last night, I am unexpectedly moved by the gesture and the tears that I have just held at bay make their way down my cheeks. As she walks away, I quickly dab again and tried to gain my composure.

As Dad gives Amelia away, on our behalf, he kisses her and returns to sit next to me. He reaches for my hand and squeezes it before gently holding it for the remainder of the service.

The nuptials, traditional in content, are beautiful. As Craig and Amelia finish their promises to each other, they both kneel while the choir sings *The Lord's Prayer*. At the close of that amazing song, Pastor James introduces them as man and wife. Craig and Amelia, both beaming, lead the wedding party back down the aisle and outside the church to host the reception line.

I follow them out of the church and for the next half hour we greet our friends and thank them for sharing this special day with us.

Later, at the reception, when the dancing begins, I watch as Amelia and Craig snuggle together, swaying to the music and whispering to each other. Andre and Adrienne are on the dance floor as well, a little less intimate, but clearly loving the early stages of their courtship. Bob and Laura, along with Robert and Caitlin each holding the hands of their children, dance together laughing and talking. Kevin and Alicia are still on the sidelines helping small children eat their cake and drink the punch.

Dad is visiting everyone and loving every minute of it. He has done so well in the weeks following Mother's death. Although he misses her, I think he is relieved not to have to watch her suffer any more.

As for me, although I have not been willing to share this day with a 'date' for the wedding, I certainly have a dance partner. I smile as John Stillman makes his way over to my table with a hand extended as an invitation to join him. I accept and stand to follow him on the dance floor.

John captured my attention the day that we met with the Carters, and we have been seeing each other quite a bit over the last month. While I am not making any commitments for now, I have experienced a stir of romance in my soul and realize that loving someone other than Roger may be a possibility. For now, let's just dance.

PART 3

Book Club Discussion

1. Becky Kennedy describes in Chapter 2 her many experiences with hospital waiting rooms. Have you ever had to sit in a hospital waiting room? Could you relate to her experiences? Discuss why and give examples of your experience.

2. Becky comforts her mother, and in turn comforts herself, by singing hymns. Growing up with her mother playing and singing hymns, this is something that they have shared together. Have you ever been in the position of needing to relate to someone very ill? If so, what did you do? Perhaps you read to them or some other method of connection? How did it make you feel to connect with them in this way?

3. In Chapter 6 Becky witnesses an experience her mother has from the other side. How do you feel when you read that? Have you or someone you know ever had an experience like this? If so, tell us about it. How do you think you would feel if you had witnessed this?

4. Becky referenced many scriptures throughout the book. In Chapter 11, she refers to James 1:2-3 as "the big one".

"²Consider it pure joy, my brothers, whenever you face trials of many kinds, ³because you know that the testing of your faith develops perseverance."

Why do you think she referenced this as "the big one"? What does this scripture say to you in the context of Soul Song? Have you considered your trials *"pure joy"*? Discuss this powerful concept as a group.

5. Amelia's role is clearly one of medical clarity and support. She and Becky are close. How would you characterize their relationship? In what way(s) is Becky's relationship different with Adrienne?

6. In Chapter 16, Becky shares her "memory bookmark" efforts to remember her mother in healthier times. That seems creative and productive given the length of the disease and the difficulty of remembering back more than twenty years to happier times. How do you think it will help her in the grief process? In the years to come? Have you been in a similar situation? What ideas/methods have you used to remember loved ones?

7. In Chapter 16 Becky's daughters love and desire to spend time with their grandmother, even when they really don't remember much about her before her illness.

(excerpt)

I watch Mother as two of her granddaughters stroke her and talk to her. Her cheeks are flushed, the fever at work. Her eyes are vacant, the look we have all come to know. Her brow is furrowed, a perpetual sign of the confusion that must dominate her days. Yet, my girls have the love and patience to be present for her. To be sensitive and caring, touching and caressing while they chatter about the stories of their grandmother that they would remember and most likely retell to their own children one day.

What about this family inspires that devotion? How does the Alzheimer's process help or hinder that attitude?

8. In Chapter 17, Becky talks to her mother and releases her to leave this earth. Later her father does the same thing. How does that make you feel? Have you ever been in that situation?

9. In Chapter 21, Dan Bridges gives his daughters and granddaughters an amazing and thoughtful gift. He personalizes a story and a piece of jewelry for each of them as a gift of remembrance for his wife Gloria. How did that make you feel? What was most touching about that experience? How do we make others feel special?

10. In Chapter 22, Adrienne finally discusses with her mother her job interview. Becky is shocked to have been left out of the loop on this opportunity. Why do you think Adrienne waited to discuss NuDawn with her mother? Have you as a parent been surprised by an adult child's choice? How did that make you feel?

11. In Chapter 23, Becky and Adrienne research human trafficking. How aware are you of this problem in the U.S.? Why do you think this topic doesn't get more attention, since it is the second largest revenue crime; behind drug trafficking?

12. In Chapter 28, Becky has some hesitation when asked to meet with the Carter family, but agrees to the meeting. An unexpected and amazing experience occurs with Deidre. Deidre has expressed her desire to become a Christian. Becky leads Deidre through a confession of faith to follow God and coordinates with Pastor James to follow that with clergy support and baptism. Why did Becky take the initiative to lead her in this confession instead of telling her to seek out a church? How would you have handled the situation? Have you had a time in your life when something that you were hesitant about doing results in something great? How did you feel?

13. In Chapter 31, Pastor James alters the worship service to provide an impromptu prayer for Adrienne's new career direction. This is a very personal approach and yet very effective in bringing the congregation together to pray for her. What did you like or dislike about this approach? When we have the opportunity to assert ourselves in prayer advocacy do we follow through?

14. At the wedding, Becky is happy for her daughter but clearly feels sad without Roger and her mother there to share the day. The emotional challenges of losing a husband unexpectedly and functioning as a care-taker for a parent for twenty-two years is overwhelming. Discuss any similar experiences that you have had? How did you cope? What comforted you? Can you relate to Becky? In what way?